PENGUIN CLASSICS

THE HISTORY OF RAS

SAMUEL JOHNSON was born in Lichfield in 1709, the son of a bookseller, and was educated at Lichfield Grammar School and, for a short time, at Pembroke College, Oxford. He taught for a while, after which he worked for a Birmingham printer, for whom he translated Jerónimo Lobo's *A Voyage to Abyssinia*. In 1735 he married Elizabeth Porter and with her money opened a boarding school. It was a failure, and in 1737 Johnson left for London. There, he became a regular contributor to the *Gentleman's Magazine* and struggled to earn a living from writing – it was not until the award of a government pension in 1762 that Johnson gained financial security.

His *London: A Poem in Imitation of the Third Satire of Juvenal* was published anonymously in 1738 and attracted some attention. *The Vanity of Human Wishes: The Tenth Satire of Juvenal Imitated* appeared under his own name in 1749. From 1750 to 1752 he issued the *Rambler*, a periodical written almost entirely by himself, and consolidated his position as a notable moral essayist with some twenty-five essays in the *Adventurer*. The *Idler* essays, lighter in tone, appeared weekly between 1758 and 1760. When his *Dictionary of the English Language* was published in 1755, Johnson took on the proportions of a literary monarch in the London of his day. In 1759 Johnson wrote *Rasselas*, reportedly completing the work in the evenings of a single week, so as to raise money to cover his mother's funeral expenses and debts. In 1763 Boswell became his follower and it is largely thanks to Boswell's *Life* that we have such intimate knowledge of Johnson. Founded in 1764, 'The Club' (of literary men) was the perfect forum for the exercise of Johnson's great conversational art. His edition of Shakespeare's plays appeared in 1765. From August to November 1773 he and Boswell toured Scotland and in 1775 his *Journey to the Western Islands of Scotland* appeared. His last major work was *Lives of the Poets* (1779–81). He died in December 1784.

PAUL GORING lectures on eighteenth-century literature and culture at the Norwegian University of Science and Technology in Trondheim. He has previously edited Laurence Sterne's *A*

Sentimental Journey through France and Italy for Penguin Classics, and his other publications include *The Rhetoric of Sensibility in Eighteenth-Century Culture* (2005).

SAMUEL JOHNSON

The History of Rasselas

Prince of Abissinia

Edited with an Introduction and Notes by
PAUL GORING

PENGUIN BOOKS

PENGUIN CLASSICS

Published by the Penguin Group
Penguin Books Ltd, 80 Strand, London WC2R ORL, England
Penguin Group (USA) Inc., 375 Hudson Street, New York, New York 10014, USA
Penguin Group (Canada), 90 Eglinton Avenue East, Suite 700, Toronto, Ontario, Canada M4P 2Y3
(a division of Pearson Penguin Canada Inc.)
Penguin Ireland, 25 St Stephen's Green, Dublin 2, Ireland
(a division of Penguin Books Ltd)
Penguin Group (Australia), 250 Camberwell Road, Camberwell, Victoria 3124, Australia
(a division of Pearson Australia Group Pty Ltd)
Penguin Books India Pvt Ltd, 11 Community Centre, Panchsheel Park, New Delhi – 110 017, India
Penguin Group (NZ), 67 Apollo Drive, Rosedale, North Shore 0632, New Zealand
(a division of Pearson New Zealand Ltd)
Penguin Books (South Africa) (Pty) Ltd, 24 Sturdee Avenue, Rosebank, Johannesburg 2196, South Africa

Penguin Books Ltd, Registered Offices: 80 Strand, London WC2R ORL, England

www.penguin.com

First published 1759
This edition first published in Penguin Classics 2007
1

Editorial material copyright © Paul Goring, 2007
All rights reserved

The moral right of the translator and editor has been asserted

Set in 10.25/12.25pt PostScript Adobe Sabon
Typeset by Rowland Phototypesetting Ltd, Bury St Edmunds, Suffolk
Printed in England by Clays Ltd, St Ives plc

Except in the United States of America, this book is sold subject
to the condition that it shall not, by way of trade or otherwise, be lent,
re-sold, hired out, or otherwise circulated without the publisher's
prior consent in any form of binding or cover other than that in
which it is published and without a similar condition including this
condition being imposed on the subsequent purchaser

ISBN: 978-0-141-43970-9

Contents

Acknowledgements

My work on this edition has been supported by a J. D. Fleeman Fellowship at the University of St Andrews. I am very grateful to the Fleeman family who established the fellowship, and to all those among the academic and administrative staff in the School of English, particularly Nick Roe and Tom Jones, and the librarians in the Special Collections department who contributed to an enjoyable and productive sojourn in Scotland. Thanks are also due to my colleagues in Trondheim, most of all Jeremy Hawthorn who, with his enviable memory for Johnson quotations and their whereabouts, has helped out on numerous occasions. For their enthusiasm for Johnson and for this edition I am grateful to Michael Goring, Claire Wakelin and Mike Gwilliam, while for support along the way and for toleration of my peripatetic working patterns I owe huge thanks to Tone Midtgård. In preparing the Notes, I have drawn upon the insights and findings of previous annotators of *Rasselas*, including George Birkbeck Hill (Oxford: Clarendon Press, 1887), J. P. Hardy (Oxford: Oxford University Press, 1968), Gwin Kolb (New Haven and London: Yale University Press, 1990) and Lynne Meloccaro (London: Everyman, 1994). Particular acknowledgement must be made to Kolb's scholarly edition, in which almost a lifetime's work on Johnson and *Rasselas* is brought together.

'It is, perhaps, not considered,' Johnson once remarked, 'through how many hands a book often passes, before it comes into those of the reader' (*Life*, p. 678). In its making this edition has passed through many hands, and I reserve my final thanks for the skilful and amiable team of editorial and production workers, particularly Lindeth Vasey, at Penguin.

Chronology

1709 *7 September** Born in Lichfield, the first child of Sarah Johnson and Michael Johnson, a bookseller and stationer. Contracts scrofula from his wet-nurse.

1712 Taken to London to be 'touched' by Queen Anne (the monarch's hands were believed to have the power to cure scrofula). Birth of brother Nathaniel.

1717 Enters Lichfield Grammar School, where he studies for over seven years.

1726 *July* Following a nine-month stay with a relative near Stourbridge, enters Stourbridge Grammar School. Returns to Lichfield and works with his father.

1728 *October* Begins studies at Pembroke College, Oxford.

1729 *December* Leaves Oxford due to poverty, without a degree, and returns to Lichfield.

1730–31 Spends grim years, suffering depression, which conclude with his father's death in December 1731.

1732 *March* Works unhappily as a schoolmaster in Market Bosworth Grammar School. *July* Returns to Lichfield, then moves to Birmingham where he works for a printer and bookseller.

1733 Observed showing signs of mental illness. Begins translation of Jerónimo Lobo's account of travels in Abyssinia.

1734 *February* Returns to Lichfield and works on several unsuccessful literary projects.

1735 *A Voyage to Abyssinia* published. Marries Elizabeth Porter née Jervis, a widow with three children. Establishes a

* Old style calendar

school near Lichfield which attracts few pupils and fails to thrive.

1737 *January* The school closes. *March* Travels to London with the future star-actor and theatre manager David Garrick, a pupil from the school. Elizabeth follows later; they live largely apart. Death of Johnson's brother. Completes his tragedy *Irene* but fails to get it staged. Writes *London*.

1738 Writes for the *Gentleman's Magazine*. *London: A Poem in Imitation of the Third Satire of Juvenal* published.

1739-45 Further attempts to become a schoolmaster, and extensive literary odd jobbing, including writing biographies and parliamentary reports.

1744 *February An Account of the Life of Mr. Richard Savage* published.

1746 Begins work on his dictionary, which occupies him for over eight years.

1749 *January The Vanity of Human Wishes: The Tenth Satire of Juvenal Imitated* published. *Irene* staged at Drury Lane (now managed by Garrick).

1750 *March* Begins writing twice-weekly issues of *Rambler*, which lasts two years and includes several short oriental tales.

1752 *March* Death of Elizabeth,

1753-4 Contributes essays to the *Adventurer*.

1755 *April A Dictionary of the English Language* published. Awarded honorary MA degree by Oxford University.

1756 Suffers serious financial problems. Edits and writes for the *Literary Magazine*, producing a number of anti-government pieces. Revives a plan for an edition of Shakespeare's works. Beginning of the Seven Years War.

1758 Begins writing weekly *Idler* essays.

1759 *January* Death of mother. Rapid composition of *Rasselas* (published 20 April). Second edition follows on 26 June. Contributes introduction to *The World Displayed*, a multi-volume collection of travel accounts.

1760 Conclusion of the *Idler*, followed by relatively low productivity for which he chastises himself.

1762 Awarded annual government pension (£300).

1763 *May* Meets James Boswell. Conclusion of the Seven Years War.

1764 Establishment of 'The Club' (later renamed 'The Literary Club'), a group of, initially, nine writers, artists and intellectuals, who meet for weekly conversation.

1765 Awarded honorary degree of LL.D. (Doctor of Laws) by Trinity College, Dublin. Edition of Shakespeare published. Becomes close friends with Henry and Hester Lynch Thrale (later Piozzi).

1766 Suffers serious depression. Spends extended periods with the Thrales and at Oxford, where, with further long visits in the coming years, he assists Robert Chambers, Professor of Law.

1769 Appointed honorary Professor in Ancient Literature by recently founded Royal Academy of Arts.

1770 *The False Alarm*, a political pamphlet in support of Parliament against John Wilkes, published. Begins revision of edition of Shakespeare.

1771 Begins revision of the *Dictionary*.

1773 Revised 4th edition of the *Dictionary* and revised edition of Shakespeare published. *August–November* Tours Scotland with James Boswell.

1774 Tours Wales with the Thrales.

1775 *A Journey to the Western Islands of Scotland* and *Taxation No Tyranny*, a pamphlet opposing American colonists' protests against taxation, published. Tours France with the Thrales. Awarded honorary Doctor of Civil Law degree by Oxford University.

1777 Begins *Lives of the Poets*.

1779 Four volumes of the *Lives* published as *Prefaces, Biographical and Critical, to the Works of the English Poets*.

1781 Six further volumes of the *Lives* published. Death of Henry Thrale.

1782–3 Suffers serious physical illness and depression.

1784 *13 December* Dies. *20 December* Buried in Westminster Abbey.

1785 James Boswell's *Journal of a Tour to the Hebrides with Samuel Johnson* published.

1786 Hester Lynch Piozzi's *Anecdotes of the late Samuel Johnson* published.

1787 Sir John Hawkins's *The Life of Samuel Johnson* published.

1791 James Boswell's *Life of Samuel Johnson* published.

Introduction

Is it possible to achieve a state of enduring earthly happiness? This is the question which *Rasselas* poses and explores. It is one of the most fundamental questions about human life which can be asked, and here it sets in motion a remarkable story of quest – a journey in pursuit of happiness – and the result is an intriguing blend of adventure and philosophical enquiry.

Rasselas was Samuel Johnson's most extensive prose fiction and it has proven to be one his most enduring and popular works, no doubt in large part due to the basic human issues it addresses and the simple appeal of its story. Johnson himself was keen to emphasize its simplicity, referring to the work as 'a little story book',[1] and when it was first published, in April 1759, it appeared before the London public in a manner which foregrounded its lighter elements. The original title was not *Rasselas*, as it has come to be known; rather the main title-page of the first edition presented it as *The Prince of Abissinia: A Tale*. 'A narrative; a story. Commonly a slight or petty account of some trifling or fabulous incident' – this was how Johnson had defined a 'tale' some years earlier in his *Dictionary of the English Language* (1755),[2] and the work does contain many of the straightforward reading pleasures suggested by that definition. (Be warned: aspects of the plot will be revealed here.) The opening chapter leads readers around Johnson's luxurious Happy Valley, a fantastical province of pleasure in which '[e]very desire' of its royal inhabitants is 'immediately granted'. Then when it emerges that the Happy Valley is, ironically, unable to sustain a permanent state of contentment, the main characters – Rasselas, his adviser Imlac, his sister Nekayah and her companion Pekuah – set off on a journey in search of real and lasting happiness. What follows is a diverse, episodic series of encounters as the travellers leave Abyssinia and journey through Egypt, meeting an array of remarkable characters and discovering many new scenes of life along the way. There is, though, much more to *Rasselas* than its simple story.

Almost all the incidents and characters generate philosophical reflection, mostly upon the nature of happiness and 'the choice of life' – a recurrent phrase in the work, which Johnson had at one stage planned to use as the title.[3] The philosophizing tendency is so strong that certain early reviewers were troubled by the work's original appearance as a light tale. Owen Ruffhead, for example, writing in the *Monthly Review* in May 1759 warned that the 'title-page will impose upon many ... fair customers, who, while they expect to frolic along the flowery paths of romance, will find themselves hoisted on metaphysical stilts, and born aloft into the regions of syllogistical subtlety, and philosophical refinement'.[4] For Ruffhead, the work seemed at first sight to be offering simply an entertaining journey of the imagination into outlandish regions – a tale of far-off royals which, he chauvinistically implies, may appeal particularly to female readers (the 'fair') in search of easy, unintellectual diversion. But the actual story, he complained, was nothing of the kind and the title was simply a misleading ruse – a sly manoeuvre by which profundity was being given the guise of exotic light reading. Fortunately for Johnson, such caveats in the reviewing magazines did little to deter the public, and *Rasselas* proved to be an instant hit. With a second printing needed just two months after the first, it was soon clear that Ruffhead had misjudged the power of the work to appeal to a vast number of readers, whether female or male, old or young, from Britain or from far beyond. By the end of the eighteenth century 28 editions had been published in Britain and Ireland; there have since been around 500 editions in English, plus over 130 in translation.[5] Ruffhead, though, was right about the essential priorities of *Rasselas*, and he was justified in pointing out that Johnson offers little in the way of flowery romance, for *Rasselas* is no typical tale of the East. In fact, what Ruffhead presents as a disturbing gap – the absence of exotic ornament – may, paradoxically, have contributed to *Rasselas*'s lasting appeal. And that disparity between the expectations set up by the work's original appearance and its rather less exotic reality can actually help us to gain insights into it and into Johnson's situation and his concerns regarding literature and the world around him as he wrote it.

Samuel Johnson and the composition of *Rasselas*

A glance at Johnson's personal circumstances when he began writing *Rasselas* suggests that he had compelling reasons for presenting his philosophical reflections in a manner which would attract a significant body of readers – or, more particularly, people who would buy the book. In 1759 Johnson was nearing fifty and had become a well-respected London author and intellectual. The son of a largely unsuccessful Lichfield bookseller, he had endured a long struggle to survive in the precarious eighteenth-century writing trade. Having had to abandon his studies at Oxford due to poverty and having failed to establish himself as a schoolmaster, Johnson had moved to London in 1737 and, while his highest ambition was to be a poet, he eked out a livelihood mainly through prodigious labours as a journalist, among other things writing reports of debates in Parliament. By the time of *Rasselas*, Johnson had been writing prolifically for over twenty years and had produced an extraordinarily vast and varied body of publications including his best-known poems, *London* (1738) and *The Vanity of Human Wishes* (1749); an outstanding work of literary biography, *An Account of the Life of Mr. Richard Savage* (1744); and a dramatic tragedy, *Irene*, which shares with *Rasselas* an Eastern setting and which was staged, with lukewarm success, at Drury Lane in 1749. He had also become known as the author of numerous essays on diverse subjects in periodicals including the *Gentleman's Magazine*, the *Adventurer* and, particularly, the *Rambler*, twice-weekly issues of which Johnson wrote almost single-handedly for two years from 1750 to 1752. He was writing weekly issues of a further periodical, the *Idler*

(1758–60), when *Rasselas* appeared, and, on top of his journalistic work, had completed the most momentous of lexicographical projects, *A Dictionary of the English Language*, between 1746 and 1755. Further works were to follow – notably his complete edition of Shakespeare's plays (1765), *A Journey to the Western Isles of Scotland* (1775) and *Lives of the Poets* (1779) – but by the time of *Rasselas* Johnson was already sufficiently renowned as a writer to have confidence that he could publish his new work anonymously and still be identified as the author. 'I will not print my name,' he wrote to his regular printer William Strahan in January 1759, 'but expect it to be known.'[6]

However, despite attaining this eminence within the literary world, Johnson had still not achieved economic security – his letter to Strahan is preoccupied with the details of the sale of *Rasselas* and it concludes with an urgent postscript: 'Get me the money if you can.'[7] Johnson's financial troubles were recurrent and long-standing, but early in 1759 he had particular pressures upon his purse due to the death in Lichfield of his mother, ninety-year-old Sarah Johnson, for whom he had retained great affection. 'You have been the best mother, and I believe the best woman in the world,' he wrote to her in her final days.[8] This loss has sometimes been called upon to explain the gloomier side of *Rasselas* – as the travellers ultimately fail to find lasting happiness, the story seems to affirm Imlac's warning to Rasselas that 'Human life is every where a state in which much is to be endured, and little to be enjoyed' (Chap. XI), and this pessimism has been seen as an effect of grief in an author who, even when not suffering personal calamities, was prone to melancholy and depression.[9] Biographically inclined reading may well detect in *Rasselas* an indirect expression of Johnson's mourning, but also on a more practical level the work can be said to owe its existence to Sarah Johnson's death, for the loss increased Johnson's financial pressures and thus spurred him on to a feat of authorship now legendary in literary history. In his *Life of Johnson*, James Boswell gives an account of the composition, reporting that 'the late Mr. Strahan the printer told me, that Johnson wrote it, that with the profits he might defray the expence of his mother's funeral, and pay some little debts which she had left . . . he composed it in the evenings of one week, sent it to the press in portions as it was written, and had never since read it over'.[10] Boswell's biography is not always strictly accurate in its detail, but there is no evidence that leads us to doubt that *Rasselas* was composed extremely rapidly or that Johnson was motivated by a pressing need for money.

Despite the circumstances of its composition *Rasselas* is no scrappy piece of commercial hack-work and as he wrote it Johnson was clearly not 'selling out' and simply reproducing the trappings of a genre of fiction which had already proved popular in the literary marketplace. *Rasselas* has become a standard example in definitions of 'potboiler', yet it is still a conscientious work, and it is also a deeply 'Johnsonian' one, in terms both of the themes it raises and of the reasoned, probing, and often droll manner in which they are explored. Johnson uses Rasselas's quest for happiness as a way of bringing up moral and philosophical concerns, almost all of which he had addressed earlier in his writing – for example, the restless nature of mankind, the differences between humans and animals, the aesthetic and social responsibilities of a writer, the pleasures and pains of marriage, and the dangers of an overactive imagination. And the voices of the characters which debate those issues, particularly that of the authoritative Imlac, are strongly reminiscent of Johnson's own distinctive voice in his non-fictional writing. Early reviewers immediately identified Johnson as the author of the anonymous work. '*The excellent Author of the* Rambler,' began a reviewer in the *London Magazine*, '*has lately obliged the World with a moral Tale, entitled* The History of Rasselas, Prince of Abyssinia [the title given at the start of the text], *in two small Pocket Volumes, which contain the most important Truths and Instructions, told in an agreeable and enchanting Manner, and in his usual nervous* [as in "sensitive"] *and sententious Stile*.'[11] The reviewer in the *Critical Review* likewise detected behind *Rasselas*, 'the learned and sensible author of the *Rambler*'.[12] More hostile commentators have long been quick to complain that the fiction is overshadowed by the looming presence of Johnson himself. 'I hardly ever hear a sentence uttered by the Princess, or the Lady Pekuah,' grumbled one critic in 1787, 'but I see the enormous Johnson in petticoats.'[13] Veiled by the fiction but not fully masked, Johnson had good reason to anticipate being identified as the author.

The Abyssinian and Egyptian settings of *Rasselas* were also, in a sense, familiar territory for Johnson. A would-be traveller frustrated by poverty, Johnson was eminently well read in accounts of the wider world, and he had made his own contributions to what was a vibrant contemporary culture of travel writing. Johnson's personal library included many works of such literature, and his first published book was a travel account: *A Voyage to Abyssinia* (1735) is a translation (from a French version) of an account by Father Jerónimo Lobo (1595–1678), a Portuguese Jesuit who spent many years in north Africa as a missionary.[14] Johnson furthermore wrote reviews of several travel works, and in the year that *Rasselas* was published he contributed an introduction to a twenty-volume collection entitled *The World Displayed; Or, A Curious Collection of Voyages and Travels*. In *Rasselas*, in fact, Johnson is not really concerned with providing an accurate depiction of the lands in which he chooses to set the tale: the Happy Valley is basically an allegorical setting, and the backdrop for the characters' journey is often only sparsely described – a characteristic which, together with the existentialist themes of the work, makes comparison with Samuel Beckett's writing quite compelling.[15] Nonetheless, Johnson doubtless drew upon his reading when conceiving the general topography of *Rasselas* and also for the depiction of certain known sites and structures, such as the pyramids of Egypt.[16]

The breakneck composition of *Rasselas*, then, was really a rapid process of intellectual and literary synthesis in which Johnson was taking materials he had gathered throughout his lifetime and was shaping them into a fictional narrative form – a quick birth after a long gestation. And the result was a work which defies easy categorization. Is *Rasselas* best described as a novel, a proto-novel, an oriental tale, a philosophic tale, an oriental philosophic tale, a moral tale, an apologue, a *conte*, a romance, a mock romance, a fable, a satire, or what? All of these terms, plus others in various combinations, have been proposed, but an uncontentious, manageable and adequately descriptive label for the work remains elusive.[17] One thing which can be agreed upon, though, is that Johnson would not have written such a work were it not for the fact that, during his lifetime, 'the Orient' had proven to be hot literary property. With its east African setting, *Rasselas* stands out from most of the eighteenth-century British fiction which is still read today. But in the eighteenth century the employment of an Eastern setting was a well-recognized literary manoeuvre, and it was one which Johnson had already tried out in a number of brief ventures into prose fiction before *Rasselas*.

Oriental tales in eighteenth-century Britain

In Britain a vogue for oriental tales spanned the eighteenth century. From the publication in English of the hugely influential *Arabian Nights' Entertainment* beginning in 1704, there followed a rash of fictional works featuring oriental locations and characters – so many that when a select collection of *Tales of the East* was compiled by Henry Weber in the early nineteenth century, it was easy to fill three vast volumes even when particularly popular examples of the genre, including *Rasselas*, were excluded 'on account of the very general diffusion of copies'.[18] Weber's collection was gathered from a broad branch of fiction comprised of both imported works and home-grown imitations. The original Arabic tales collected as the *Arabian Nights' Entertainment* came to British readers via a French translation by Antoine Galland (nineteen English editions of the multi-volume collection would be published by the end of the century). A similar route was taken by another influential collection of Eastern stories, *The Thousand and One Days: Persian Tales* (1714), which was translated from the French by Ambrose Philips. Among other exotic titles coming to Britain from France were *Turkish Tales* (1708), *Chinese Tales* (1725) and *Mogul Tales; or, The Dreams of Men Awake* (1736). British

authors were quick to capitalize on the popularity of such
works. For a 1711 issue of the *Spectator*, for example, Joseph
Addison wrote 'The Vision of Mirzah' – a magical moral tale set
in the hills of 'Bagdat', which Addison presented as a translation
from an original oriental manuscript picked up in Cairo.[19] Traditionally short, such tales were well suited for periodical publication and further examples appeared in the *Spectator*, the
Guardian and other magazines. Johnson published his first
oriental tales in 1750 – he devoted four numbers of the *Rambler*
to individual tales before then attempting a more expansive
work, 'The history of Seged', which appeared in two consecu-
tive instalments.[20] Set in Abyssinia and with a protagonist in
search of happiness, 'Seged' bears significant comparison with
Rasselas and can in many ways be seen as a precursor. Johnson's
subsequent short oriental fiction would appear in the *Idler*;
while he did not write similar works for the *Adventurer*
(1752–4), his collaborator and the magazine's main author,
John Hawkesworth, did, and, according to an early biographer
of Johnson, it was due to the success of Hawkesworth's stories
as well as those in the *Rambler* that Johnson began 'meditating
a fictitious history, of a greater extent than any that had
appeared in either of those papers'.[21]

The appeal and popularity of many oriental tales clearly
rested upon their offering eighteenth-century readers the excite-
ment of vicarious adventure and the opportunity to indulge in
exotic fantasy worlds far removed from the everyday realities
of European life. Often their plots are rich in incident and
danger; they present a range of remarkable Eastern characters,
many of them racial stereotypes to which it is now easy to
object; they include lavish descriptions of sumptuous environ-
ments; and they are regularly enlivened by supernatural para-
phernalia – genies, demons, dream visions, and magical charms
and spells. Johnson gestures towards the lavishness of such
fiction through his creation of the Happy Valley 'surrounded
on every side by mountains, of which the summits overhang
the middle part', with its only entrance 'closed with gates of
iron, forged by the artificers of ancient days, so massy that no
man could, without the help of engines, open or shut them' (I).

The fauna of the valley is also rich and fanciful – the valley's central lake is 'inhabited by fish of every species, and frequented by every fowl whom nature has taught to dip the wing in water', while wandering on the land are '[a]ll animals that bite the grass, or brouse the shrub, whether wild or tame ... secured from beasts of prey by the mountains which confined them' (I). However, as Owen Ruffhead was keen to stress, *Rasselas* does stand out as a notably unexotic work when compared with many of its peers. Johnson offers no flying carpets – only an impractical flying machine which, as it plummets straight into the lake on its maiden flight, might well be seen as emblematic of the down-to-earth realities of existence with which *Rasselas* is primarily concerned (VI). It was not uncommon for oriental fictions to be, like *Rasselas*, intellectually engaged and attentive to serious topics: the *Arabian Nights* and *Persian Tales* include passages of moral, philosophical and social observation, and many of the tales they inspired, such as Addison's 'The Vision of Mirzah', exhibit clear moral or philosophical ends.[22] Ruffhead, then, was exaggerating the flowery hollowness of typical oriental fantasies in order to make his contrast, but it is true that these works typically adorn their intellectual concerns with an Eastern garb more elaborate than what we find in *Rasselas*. How can *Rasselas*'s distinctiveness be accounted for? At least part of the answer lies in Johnson's firm beliefs concerning the nature of good literature and the manner in which the human imagination should be stimulated by literary representations.

Great thoughts and the dangers of fiction

'Great thoughts are always general,' Johnson wrote in his life of the poet Abraham Cowley. They consist, he went on, 'in positions not limited by exceptions, and in descriptions not descending to minuteness'.[23] The idea of the superiority of the general over the particular was central to Johnson's work as both a critic and a writer of literature, and it can help to explain why *Rasselas* does not encourage deep absorption and indulgence in its settings, for Johnson typically followed his own precepts and avoided 'descending to minuteness' in his descriptive passages. A sense of stateliness in *Rasselas*, with the text exhibiting an almost biblical grandeur, is created through an emphasis upon general terms, with very few specific objects actually being named. For example, in the account of the Happy Valley we read of 'tables covered with luxury' (II), but are given no further elaboration upon the nature of that luxury. Similarly when the travellers reach Cairo, we read of 'merchants' and '[c]ommerce' (XVI), but we are given no details of the type of commerce – the sparse, non-specific description of Cairo could apply to almost any large commercial city. Johnson actually presents within *Rasselas* a rationale for this tendency by introducing the topics of literary composition and the ethical duties of an author into a conversation between Imlac and Rasselas. In a much-quoted passage he has Imlac – who, of all the characters, most often seems to take on the function of authorial spokesman – declare that 'The business of the poet . . . is to examine, not the individual, but the species; to remark general properties and large appearances: he does not number the streaks of the tulip, or describe the different shades in the verdure of the forest' (X).[24] Aspiring to this ideal himself, Johnson produced a story which tends not to draw readers into a world of fictional detail, but rather operates on a level of generalities at one remove from the representation of specific things.

Imlac's remarks on the duties of an author suggest the deliberation which lay behind Johnson's providing in *Rasselas* something other than an escapist fantasy, and when considering Johnson as an author of fiction it is important also to remember that even though he wrote fiction he was fundamentally suspicious of the whole enterprise of fictional representation and he was prominent as a self-appointed arbiter of the uses to which fiction should be put by individual readers and society more generally. He frequently expressed a profound wariness of the human imagination in an uncontrolled state and of the capacity of literary fiction to induce mental disturbance – all readers, so far as Johnson was concerned, were capable of following Don Quixote's journey through fiction and into madness. In a well-known essay in the *Rambler*, for example,

Johnson warned of the power of fiction to take hold of a reader's mind – to 'take possession of the memory by a kind of violence, and produce effects almost without the intervention of the will'.[25] It is a concern which is explored in *Rasselas* and which may be said to underlie its reserved depiction of the East. Several of the characters encountered by the travellers are afflicted with quixotic obsessions and delusions, most notably an astonomer 'who has spent forty years in unwearied attention to the motions and appearances of the celestial bodies' (XL). His compulsive study has caused him to believe that he can actually control the 'weather, and the distribution of the seasons' (XLI), a mad fantasy which leads Imlac to conclude that 'Of the uncertainties of our present state, the most dreadful and alarming is the uncertain continuance of reason' (XLIII). The case history of the astronomer, in fact, provides the foundation for *Rasselas*'s fullest and most explicit treatment of mental derangement in a chapter entitled 'The dangerous prevalence of imagination' (XLIV). This chapter consists largely of a lecture to Rasselas and Nekayah by Imlac, who, while not discussing literary fiction *per se*, nonetheless presents a warning against the excessive exercise of the imagination through indulgence in unreality which reflects Johnson's owns concerns about certain types of literary fiction. 'There is no man,' Imlac states,

> whose imagination does not sometimes predominate over his reason . . . No man will be found in whose mind airy notions do not sometimes tyrannise . . . All power of fancy over reason is a degree of insanity . . . To indulge the power of fiction, and send imagination out upon the wing, is often the sport of those who delight too much in silent speculation . . . By degrees the reign of fancy is confirmed; she grows first imperious, and in time despotic. Then fictions begin to operate as realities, false opinions fasten upon the mind, and life passes in dreams of rapture or of anguish.

Through Imlac's lecture, *Rasselas* can be said to present not only a stark portrait of psychological misrule but also a justification of its own tendency to block the indulgence of the imagination. Like Imlac, Johnson was mistrustful of the type of imaginative 'frolic' which, as Ruffhead's review suggests, some readers might have expected on seeing the work's title, and so it is no surprise to find him avoiding it in *Rasselas*. Johnson may well have been pleased to have it confirmed that readers were not swept off into realms of oriental fantasy, and that the philosophical elements of his work stood firm in the foreground of readers' experiences of the work.

Johnson and European imperialism

The way in which the Orient is depicted in *Rasselas* can also, though, be said to have an ideological basis – it may be seen as an implicit intervention in debates concerning Europe's relationship with the wider world which, in a period of avid global exploration and imperial advancement, typically re-volved around a deep-seated belief in European racial and cul-tural superiority. As has been vigorously argued by Edward Said, particularly in his influential *Orientalism: Western Con-ceptions of the Orient* (1978), and by many other post-colonial historians and critics, Europeans from the Renaissance onwards produced a mass of derogatory representations of the East which collectively served to construct a powerful and wide-spread image of the Orient as a dangerous and uncivilized zone lacking – among other 'civilized' qualities – rationality, morality, sexual restraint and proper religion. Johnson's work stands out by resisting such stereotyping – indeed in *Rasselas* and elsewhere in his writing we can find a bold refusal to brand the non-European world as racially and culturally backward. Johnson was a committed essentialist: his writing contains numerous expressions of the contention that 'human nature is always the same',[26] and that, as Imlac tells Rasselas, there are certain 'general and transcendental truths, which will always be the same' (X). And such a belief in a universal state of being which transcends racial difference underlies the manner in which Johnson represents non-European cultures and peoples. In *Rasselas* we meet no savages, noble or otherwise. Rather Johnson's characters are endowed with those qualities of civility, rationality, morality and erotic continence which many other representations of the time were highlighting as the very things that non-Europeans lacked. And while Johnson was a committed Christian, he is not concerned with the promotion of his own religion in the work. Beginning in Abyssinia, the only Christian country in that region of east Africa, *Rasselas* may have delivered a bracing reminder to Christian readers in Europe of the Middle Eastern origins of their own religion,[27] but what is perhaps more important is that the narrative does not draw attention to religious differences when the travellers reach non-Christian Egypt. Johnson is concerned with what humans have in common, not those circumstances and institutions which separate them.

There is one section where it seems as though Johnson is on the brink of reproducing a standard oriental stereotype. This is the sequence of scenes in which Pekuah and two maids are abducted by a troop of Arabs and held for ransom in the seraglio of their chief. Seraglio scenes were common in oriental tales, and some readers may well have been expecting at this point a lurid tale of seduction or sexual assault by a rampant and lascivious Arab – if so, they were to be soon disappointed. The chief is a warrior but he is a highly civilized and honest one: 'I am not one of the lawless and cruel rovers of the desert; I know the rules of civil life,' he says (XXXVIII). And as a sexual being he turns out to be really quite dull – he is bored by the women in the seraglio and he makes no seductive advances towards Pekuah. His nocturnal activity with her takes another form: 'At night,' Pekuah relates, 'the Arab always attended me to a tower set apart for celestial observations, where he endeavoured to teach me the names and courses of the stars' (XXXIX). For a moment it seems as though the story might take an erotic turn, but we end up instead with a lesson in astronomy.

A number of readers certainly have been surprised and troubled by the manner in which Johnson represents the Orient – none more so than the nineteenth-century imperialist politician and historian Thomas Babington Macaulay (1800–1859), whose ardent sense of racial difference and of European superiority rendered *Rasselas* more or less intolerable. For Macaulay, writing an 1856 entry for the *Encyclopedia Britannica*, Johnson had produced in *Rasselas* merely a dislocated image of home:

> What a real company of Abyssinians would have been may be learned from Bruce's Travels.[28] But Johnson, not content with turning filthy savages ignorant of their letters, and gorged with raw steaks cut from living cows, into philosophers as eloquent and enlightened as himself or his friend Burke, and into ladies as highly accomplished as Mrs. Lennox or Mrs. Sheridan, transferred the whole domestic system of England to Egypt. Into a land of harems, a land of polygamy, a land where women are married without ever being seen, he introduced the flirtations and jealousies of our ball-rooms. In a land where there is boundless liberty of divorce, wedlock is described as the indissoluble compact.[29]

Macaulay dismisses *Rasselas* as a failure of representation founded on ignorance and misunderstanding of the wider world – if he recognizes in the work a criticism of the imperialist ideology which was burgeoning in Johnson's time and was more or less at its height in his own, he does not acknowledge it. More recent critics, though, have been inclined to detect such criticism in *Rasselas*, and to see the pounding essentialism of the work as an expression of Johnson's hostility towards imperialism and to the rhetoric of racial difference by which European colonial expansion was being justified as a type of civilizing project.[30] *Rasselas* is set at no specific time, but it was written at a key moment in the development of the British empire – in the midst of the Seven Years War (1756–63), at the beginning of a remarkable year in which Britain was to defeat France in hard-fought campaigns on fronts in India, Canada, Germany and the West Indies and thus effectively establish British supremacy over much of the globe.[31] Johnson was openly critical of European imperial practices: he used his introduction to *The World Displayed*, published in December 1759, as an occasion to condemn the way in which colonized peoples were systematically viewed and treated. Of a report of the murderous manner of early Portuguese colonization, he writes

> We are openly told, that they had the less scruple concerning their treatment of the savage people, because they scarcely considered them as distinct from beasts; and indeed the practice of all the *European* nations, and among others of the *English* barbarians that cultivate the southern islands of *America* proves, that this opinion, however absurd and foolish, however wicked and injurious, still continues to prevail.[32]

Recognizing Johnson's ingrained resistance to ideas of racial hierarchy is important for it helps us to understand his representation in *Rasselas* of the Orient and its peoples as pointedly civilized. Johnson was not naively transplanting the 'whole domestic system of England' to Egypt, as Macaulay would have it. His non-European characters are not misplaced Europeans, but they resemble rational, civilized Europeans for the reason that Johnson does not recognize any essential difference between the two. Such thinking implicitly informs the broad manner of representation in *Rasselas*, but it also emerges explicitly when the work probes, albeit fleetingly, the reasons behind the imbalance of power in the world. During one of the many conversation scenes, Rasselas asks Imlac, 'By what means . . . are the Europeans thus powerful? or why, since they can so easily visit Asia and Africa for trade or conquest, cannot the Asiaticks and Africans invade their coasts, plant colonies in their ports, and give laws to their natural princes? The same wind that carries them back would bring us thither' (XI). Imlac's response is not altogether straightforward: 'They are more powerful, Sir, than we . . . because they are wiser; knowledge will always predominate over ignorance, as man governs the other animals. But why their knowledge is more than ours, I know not what reason can be given, but the unsearchable will of the Supreme Being.' Is Imlac suggesting that the Europeans are *by nature* wiser, or that they are simply the beneficiaries of a greater accumulation of knowledge? The latter reading – supported by Johnson's *Dictionary*'s definition of 'wise' as 'having practical knowledge' – is the more valid here, especially given the way in which the passage develops with Imlac's consideration of why 'their knowledge is more than ours'. For Imlac, a 'Supreme Being' may, for reasons unknowable, have countenanced an uneven international distribution of knowledge and thereby power, but *essentially* the peoples of the world are on a level.[33]

Rasselas beyond its historical moment

The nature of *Rasselas* can be illuminated by seeing the work as a response to imperialist ideology in general and to the Seven Years War in particular, but *Rasselas* is also more than that. If we are to account for why the work has maintained its power for so long, we must look beyond its political resonance in its own time and return to Johnson's attempt to uncover timeless human essentials and to comment upon the most fundamental aspects of human experience, for it is this which has sustained the work's appeal – even as post-structuralist and post-modernist thought casts widespread suspicion upon the very idea of human essentiality. While other oriental fictions have been forgotten, *Rasselas*, with its unconcern for human specificity and difference, has continued to attract readers of all kinds. Many feminist critics, for example, have been drawn to the work since Johnson's essentialism crosses boundaries not only of race but also of sex, and the female characters show no less strength and intellectual capacity than the male characters – in *Rasselas*, men and women are equals in the predicament of life.[34] Playing out an allegory of the human condition, Johnson's characters can invite easy identification, and critics who complain that *Rasselas* has no proper characters – that characterization was beyond Johnson's literary capabilities – actually touch upon a reason for the work's appeal, for it is because the characters are not encrusted with such details as are found in more realist fictions that their fundamental situation can be so readily recognized and identified with by readers. What type of commentary on human life, then, does *Rasselas* offer readers?

As we have seen, *Rasselas* displays a diverse range of philosophical concerns, but the overarching matter it examines is the nature of earthly happiness. Is it possible, the work asks, to take action – to make a 'choice of life' – which will result in lasting happiness? And crucial to the way in which this question is explored is the Johnsonian view of the human imagination as the source of insatiable desires for novelty and variety. The 'state of life,' Nekayah declares, is such that 'none are happy but by the anticipation of change: the change itself is nothing; when we have made it, the next wish is to change again' (XLVII). Life, for Johnson, is a condition of constant mental restlessness – a condition in which desires might be satisfied but only momentarily, for on the tail of every satisfaction comes a new awareness of the vacuity of life and with it the need for new desires and new satisfactions. This is why the pleasures of the Happy Valley grow stale; this is why Rasselas and his companions must escape its confines and pursue their search for happiness elsewhere.

Ultimately *Rasselas* does not answer the main question it poses – its exploration of a series of different ways of living is brought to a close in a 'conclusion, in which nothing is concluded' (XLIX). At the end of the story the travellers have failed to identify a settled state of existence which can provide enduring satisfaction, and as they resolve to return to Abyssinia (whether to seek re-entry into the Happy Valley or not is unclear) the work appears to confirm the point of Johnson's earlier poem on 'The Vanity of Human Wishes' and of Ecclesiastes 2:11 that life is filled with 'vanity and vexation of spirit'.[35] *Rasselas* does not, then, offer any real guidance about the 'choice of life' – overall it is not an obviously instructive work, although along the way it contains didactically inclined passages. Some readers and critics have suggested that the work *does* have a clear lesson – that, as Boswell put it, 'Johnson meant, by shewing the unsatisfactory nature of things temporal, to direct the hopes of man to things eternal',[36] but whether the work can really be said to advance such a view of the afterlife is open to question. Certainly specific points in the story can be identified to support such a view. For example, at the end of the penultimate chapter – a discourse 'on the nature of the soul' (XLVIII) – Nekayah announces that 'the choice of life is become less important; I hope hereafter to think only on the choice of eternity'. Had the work ended at this point it could be very tempting to follow the optimistic school of interpretation represented by Boswell and to see Nekayah's remark as a type of concluding moral which might be separated from the speaking character and allowed to stand as an axiom authorized by the work itself. But those words *are* the words of a character, and there is nothing in the text which truly suggests that readers should interpret them in any other way. Added to which the work does not end here, and in the inconclusive conclusion that follows there is a further stark reminder that whatever 'schemes of happiness' might be conjured up by the travellers 'none could be obtained' (XLIX). This overriding emphasis upon the impossibility of earthly happiness, together with the uncertain authority of the work's remarks on the soul and the afterlife, suggest an interpretation quite contrary to Boswell's – a pessimistic interpretation, which, like the opposite reading, has a long heritage, reaching back at least to Sir John Hawkins, who, in his biography of Johnson, remarked of *Rasselas* that 'it cannot be said, that it vindicates the ways of God to man'.[37]

One thing that this particular point of disagreement has made very clear is that *neither* position can be said to be explicitly and unambiguously advanced by *Rasselas* – no clear doctrine regarding the afterlife can be unproblematically extracted.[38] The fictional form chosen by Johnson, in fact, renders the work as a whole far from doctrinaire. The first sentence, with its bold address to 'Ye who listen with credulity to the whispers of fancy, and persue with eagerness the phantoms of hope', appears to be establishing a voice of authority in the text, but that voice is not sustained, and subsequently the function of the narrator is largely reduced to scene setting and the direction of the action. The philosophical content emerges, therefore, not so much from the single voice of the narrator as from the characters – it is splintered and divided among a range of fictional voices which between them perform a type of dramatized philosophical dialogue or debate. The distinctive voice of Johnson may be 'heard' emerging from each of the main characters, but it emerges in a fragmented form as an extended *conversation* – as a dialogue peppered with questions, responses, more questions, and so on. Johnson practises a type of multiple ventriloquism in *Rasselas* and the result is not so much a treatise cloaked in fiction as a sceptical enquiry.[39] *Rasselas* describes and is itself an intellectual expedition; it is a pursuit which does not reach a clear conclusion but which – for Johnson, for his characters and for readers – enables, temporarily at least, the vacuity of life to be filled and the hunger of the imagination to be satisfied.

NOTES

For short citations, see list of Abbreviations, p. 113.

1. Letter to Lucy Porter, 23 March 1759, *The Letters of Samuel Johnson, Volume I: 1731–1772*, ed. Bruce Redford (Oxford: Clarendon Press, 1992), p. 184 (hereafter *Letters*).
2. *Dictionary*.
3. 'The title will be The choice of Life or The History of — Prince of Abissinia' (letter to his printer William Strahan, 20 January 1759, *Letters*, p. 178).
4. Owen Ruffhead, *Monthly Review*, no. 20 (May 1759), p. 437.
5. Editions of *Rasselas* up to 1984 are catalogued in J. D. Fleeman's *A Bibliography of the Works of Samuel Johnson*, 2 vols. (Oxford: Clarendon Press, 2000), I, pp. 785–989.
6. Letter to William Strahan, 20 January 1759, *Letters*, p. 179.
7. Ibid., p. 179.
8. Letter to Sarah Johnson, 20 January 1759, *Letters*, p. 177.
9. Such a view of *Rasselas* has a long history. See, for example, Sir John Hawkins's account of how Johnson 'poured out his sorrow in gloomy reflection, and being destitute of comfort himself, described the world as nearly without it' (*The Life of Samuel Johnson* (London: 1787), p. 367).
10. *Life*, pp. 240–41.
11. *London Magazine*, no. 28 (May 1759), p. 258.
12. *Critical Review*, no. 7 (April 1759), p. 373.

13. William Hayley, *Two Dialogues; Containing A Comparative View of the Lives, Characters, and Writings, of Philip, The Late Earl of Chesterfield, and Dr. Samuel Johnson* (London: 1787), p. 106.

14. On Johnson's library, see Donald Greene, *Samuel Johnson's Library: An Annotated Guide* (Victoria, BC: English Literary Studies, University of Victoria, 1975) and J. D. Fleeman, *The sale catalogue of Samuel Johnson's library: a facsimile edition, with an introduction and notes* (Victoria, BC: English Literary Studies, University of Victoria, 1975).

15. W. K. Wimsatt draws persuasive comparisons between Johnson and Beckett in 'In Praise of *Rasselas*: Four Notes (Converging)', in *Imagined Worlds: Essays in Honour of John Butt*, ed. Maynard Mack and Ian Gregor (London: Methuen, 1968), pp. 111–36, and a more recent discussion is in Frederik N. Smith, 'Johnson, Beckett, and the "Choice of Life"', *The Age of Johnson: A Scholarly Annual*, 9 (1998), pp. 187–200.

16. On Johnson's use of travel literature as source material for *Rasselas*, two articles stand out for their meticulous and scholarly approach: Donald M. Lockhart, '"The Fourth Son of the Mighty Emperor": The Ethiopian Background of Johnson's *Rasselas*', *PMLA*, 78 (1963), pp. 516–28, and Arthur J. Weitzman, 'More Light on *Rasselas*: The Background of the Egyptian Episodes', *Philological Quarterly*, 48:1 (1969), pp. 42–58. See also Thomas Curley's *Samuel Johnson and the Age of Travel* (Athens: University of Georgia Press, 1976), pp. 147–82 – Curley overstates the geographical accuracy to which Johnson aspired, but his study arrives at some interesting conclusions regarding Johnson's absorption and transformation of earlier travel writing in his 'fable of moral pilgrimage' (p. 149).

17. The question of the generic identity of *Rasselas* has been addressed in many studies, and Gwin Kolb includes a useful summation of the debate in his introduction to *Rasselas and Other Tales*, ed. Gwin J. Kolb, The Yale Edition of the Works of Samuel Johnson, vol. XVI (New Haven and London: Yale University Press, 1990), pp. xxxiii–xliv.

18. *Tales of the East*, ed. Henry Weber, 3 vols. (Edinburgh: 1812), I, p. lxii.

19. *Spectator*, no. 159, 1 September 1711.

20. *Rambler*, nos. 38 (28 July 1750), 65 (30 October 1750), 120 (11 May 1751), 190 (11 January 1752), 204 (29 February 1752) and 205 (3 March 1752), in *Rambler*, III, pp. 205–10, III,

pp. 344–9, IV, pp. 275–80, V, pp. 228–33, V, pp. 296–300, and V, pp. 300–305 respectively.

21. Hawkins, *Life of Samuel Johnson*, p. 366. Johnson's oriental tales for the *Idler* appear in nos. 75 (22 September 1759), 99 (8 March 1760) and 101 (22 March 1760), in *Idler*, pp. 232–5, pp. 302–5, and pp. 309–11 respectively.

22. For a discussion of the genre which highlights its moral and philosophical tendencies, see Arthur Weitzman, 'The Oriental Tale in the Eighteenth Century: A Reconsideration', *Studies on Voltaire in the Eighteenth Century*, 58 (1967), pp. 1839–55.

23. Samuel Johnson, *Lives of the English Poets*, ed. George Birkbeck Hill, 3 vols. (Oxford: Clarendon Press, 1905), I, p. 21.

24. Irvin Ehrenpreis, among many other critics, argues for the 'congruence of Imlac's opinions with those of the middle-aged Johnson; for on moral, literary and philosophical subjects we can normally take him as the author's spokesman. Even when Johnson pokes fun at Imlac, we may suppose he is laughing at himself' ('*Rasselas* and some meanings of "structure" in literary criticism', *Novel*, 14:2 (1981), pp. 101–17). For alternative views, see note 1 to Chap. X.

25. No. 4 (31 March 1750), *Rambler*, III, p. 22.

26. *Adventurer*, no. 99 (16 October 1753), in *Adventurer*, II, p. 431.

27. This point is made in a perceptive and informative essay by Clement Hawes, where it is argued that 'Johnson picked the setting of Coptic Christianity in the highlands of Ethiopia as a way of reminding his Protestant readers of Christianity's location, during its formative years, in the deserts of West Asia and North Africa' ('Johnson and imperialism', in *The Cambridge Companion to Samuel Johnson*, ed. Greg Clingham (Cambridge: Cambridge University Press, 1997), p. 116).

28. Macaulay refers to James Bruce's account of his travels in Abyssinia between 1768 and 1773 to discover the source of the Nile. Several editions and abridgements of Bruce's work had been published by Macaulay's time.

29. Thomas Babington Macaulay, 'Life of Johnson', in Samuel Johnson, *Prose & Poetry with Boswell's Character, Macaulay's Life and Raleigh's Essay*, ed. R. W. Chapman (Oxford: Clarendon Press, 1922), pp. 28–9. Johnson was well acquainted with the philosopher Edmund Burke (1729–97); the novelist Charlotte Lennox (*c.* 1729–1804) and Frances Sheridan (1724–66), playwright and novelist.

30. See Hawes, 'Johnson and imperialism'; Steven Scherwatzky,

'Johnson, *Rasselas*, and the politics of empire', *Eighteenth-Century Life*, 16:3 (1992), pp. 103–13; and Charles Campbell, 'Johnson's Arab: Anti-Orientalism in *Rasselas*', *Abhath al-Yarmouk* (*Literature & Linguistics*), 12:1 (1994), pp. 51–66.

31. On the importance of the events of this particular year, see Frank McLynn, *1759: The Year Britain Became Master of the World* (London: Jonathan Cape, 2004).

32. *The World Displayed; Or, A Curious Collection of Voyages and Travels*, 20 vols. (London: 1759), I, p. xiv.

33. Boswell reports Johnson rereading *Rasselas* in 1781: 'he seemed to be intensely fixed; having told us, that he had not looked at it since it was first published. I happened to take it out of my pocket this day, and he seized upon it with avidity.' Pointing to Imlac's response to Rasselas's question, Johnson said 'This, Sir, no man can explain otherwise' (*Life*, p. 1156).

34. See, for example, Marlene R. Hansen, 'Sex and love, marriage and friendship: a feminist reading of the quest for happiness in *Rasselas*', *English Studies* 66:6 (1985), pp. 513–25; Tara Ghoshal Wallace, ' "Guarded with fragments": body and discourse in *Rasselas*', *South Central Review*, 9:4 (1992), pp. 31–45; and Roslyn Reso Foy, 'Johnson's *Rasselas*: women in the "stream of life" ', *English Language Notes*, 32:1 (1994), pp. 39–53.

35. The connection with Ecclesiastes (Authorized Version) is noted by Boswell (*Life*, p. 241).

36. *Life*, p. 242.

37. Hawkins, *Life of Samuel Johnson*, p. 370. For a valuable discussion of the 'hopeful' and 'hopeless' schools of interpretation, see Duane H. Smith, 'Repetitive patterns in Samuel Johnson's *Rasselas*,' *Studies in English Literature 1500–1900*, 36:3 (1996), pp. 623–39. Smith argues that 'rather than directing our attention to eternal life or pointing out the essential nihilism of life, as critics have repeatedly argued, Johnson presents a narrative that functions for us as readers in much the same way as the many activities of Rasselas and Nekayah: they divert attention from fear and boredom and provide some measure of entertainment' (p. 624).

38. In his study of criticism of *Rasselas*, Edward Tomarken similarly concludes that 'the religious question cannot be resolved' (*Johnson, 'Rasselas', and the Choice of Criticism* (Lexington: University Press of Kentucky, 1989), p. 36).

39. Fred Parker sees the work in this way in 'The skepticism of
     Johnson's *Rasselas*', in *The Cambridge Companion to Samuel
     Johnson*, pp. 127–42.

Further Reading

EDITION

The standard scholarly edition of *Rasselas* is
Rasselas and Other Tales, ed. Gwin J. Kolb, The Yale Edition
  of the Works of Samuel Johnson, vol. XVI (New Haven and
  London: Yale University Press, 1990).

RECEPTION AND CRITICAL HISTORY

On Johnson's general reception and critical history
Boulton, James T. (ed.), *Johnson: The Critical Heritage*
  (London: Routledge and Kegan Paul, 1971).
Lynn, Steven, 'Johnson's critical reception', in *The Cambridge
  Companion to Samuel Johnson*, ed. Clingham, pp. 240–53.
For works specifically on *Rasselas*'s reception and critical
  history
Kolb, Gwin J., 'The Early Reception of *Rasselas*, 1759–1800',
  in *Greene Centennial Studies: Essays Presented to Donald
  Greene in the Centennial Year of the University of Southern
  California*, ed. Paul J. Korshin and Robert R. Allen (Char-
  lottesville: University Press of Virginia, 1984), pp. 217–49.
  (Much of this work is also presented in Kolb's edition of
  Rasselas.)
Tomarken, Edward, *Johnson, 'Rasselas', and the Choice of
  Criticism* (Lexington: University Press of Kentucky, 1989).

SELECTED CRITICAL WORKS
ADDRESSING *RASSELAS*

There is a large body of criticism, and this list presents some of the more influential and/or thought-provoking interventions into the major debates concerning *Rasselas*'s sources and contexts, its structure, its interpretation as optimistic or pessimistic, and the politics of the work.

Baker, Sheridan, '*Rasselas*: Psychological Irony and Romance', *Philological Quarterly*, 45 (1966), pp. 249–61.

Curley, Thomas, *Samuel Johnson and the Age of Travel* (Athens: University of Georgia Press, 1976), chapter 5.

Damrosch, Leopold, Jr., 'Johnson's *Rasselas*: Limits of Wisdom, Limits of Art', in *Augustan Studies: Essays in Honor of Irvin Ehrenpreis*, ed. Douglas Lane Patey and Timothy Keegan (Newark: University of Delaware Press, 1985), pp. 205–14.

Ehrenpreis, Irvin, '*Rasselas* and some meanings of "structure" in literary criticism', *Novel: a forum on fiction*, 14:2 (1981), pp. 101–17.

Hansen, Marlene R., 'Sex and love, marriage and friendship: a feminist reading of the quest for happiness in *Rasselas*', *English Studies: a journal of English language and literature*, 66:6 (1985), pp. 513–25.

Hawes, Clement, 'Johnson and imperialism', in *The Cambridge Companion to Samuel Johnson*, ed. Clingham, pp. 114–26.

Hudson, Nicholas, '"Open" and "Enclosed" Readings of *Rasselas*', *The Eighteenth Century: Theory and Interpretation*, 31:1 (1990), pp. 47–67.

Jones, Emrys L., 'The Artistic Form of *Rasselas*', *Review of English Studies*, 18 (1967), pp. 387–401.

Kolb, Gwin J., 'The Structure of *Rasselas*', *PMLA*, 66 (1951), pp. 698–717.

Lockhart, Donald M., '"The Fourth Son of the Mighty Emperor": The Ethiopian Background of Johnson's *Rasselas*', *PMLA*, 78 (1963), pp. 516–28.

McIntosh, Carey, *The Choice of Life: Samuel Johnson and the World of Fiction* (New Haven and London: Yale University Press, 1973), especially chapter 6.

Parke, Catherine N., 'Rasselas and the conversation of history', *Age of Johnson*, 1 (1987), pp. 79–109.

Parker, Fred, 'The skepticism of Johnson's *Rasselas*', in *The Cambridge Companion to Samuel Johnson*, ed. Clingham, pp. 127–42.

Preston, Thomas R., 'The Biblical Context of Johnson's *Rasselas*', *PMLA*, 84 (1969), pp. 274–81.

Scherwatzky, Steven, 'Johnson, *Rasselas*, and the politics of empire', *Eighteenth-Century Life*, 16:3 (1992), pp. 103–13.

Sherburn, George, 'Rasselas Returns – to What?', *Philological Quarterly*, 38 (1959), pp. 383–4.

Smith, Duane H., 'Repetitive patterns in Samuel Johnson's *Rasselas*', *Studies in English Literature 1500–1900*, 36:3 (1996), pp. 623–39.

Wallace, Tara Ghoshal, ' "Guarded with fragments": body and discourse in *Rasselas*', *South Central Review*, 9:4 (1992), pp. 31–45.

Weinbrot, Howard, 'The Reader, the General and the Particular: Johnson and Imlac in Chapter Ten of *Rasselas*', *Eighteenth-Century Studies*, 5 (1971), pp. 80–96.

Weitzman, Arthur J., 'More Light on *Rasselas*: The Background of the Egyptian Episodes', *Philological Quarterly*, 48:1 (1969), pp. 42–58.

ON JOHNSON

Bate, Walter Jackson, *Samuel Johnson* (New York: Harcourt Brace Jovanovich, 1977; London: Chatto and Windus, 1978). An important psychoanalytically inclined biography.

Boswell, James, *The Life of Samuel Johnson*, ed. R. W. Chapman (Oxford and New York: Oxford University Press, 1980). Among biographical accounts, Boswell's still stands out, and is readily available in the Oxford World's Classics series. The standard scholarly edition, edited by G. B. Hill and revised by L. F. Powell, was published by the Clarendon Press (1934–64).

Clifford, James L., *Young Sam Johnson* (New York: McGraw-Hill, 1955).

—, *Dictionary Johnson: Samuel Johnson's Middle Years* (New York: McGraw-Hill, 1979). Both of Clifford's books concern Johnson's dealings with the book trade.

Clingham, Greg (ed.), *The Cambridge Companion to Samuel Johnson* (Cambridge: Cambridge University Press, 1997). A good general overview of Johnson's writing, life, beliefs, and position within his own time and within literary history.

DeMaria, Robert, *The Life of Samuel Johnson: A Critical Biography* (Oxford: Blackwell, 1993). Focuses on Johnson as a scholar.

Kaminski, Thomas, *The Early Career of Samuel Johnson* (New York and Oxford: Oxford University Press, 1987). A scrupulous study of Johnson's work in London from 1737 to 1746.

Wain, John, *Samuel Johnson: A Biography* (London: Macmillan, 1974). A general and very readable account.

BIBLIOGRAPHIES OF JOHNSON'S WORKS AND OF SECONDARY CRITICISM

For further study of Johnson, there are several excellent bibliographies which ease any attempt to navigate the oceans of primary works and criticism. Regarding his works, including editions up to 1984, the following monumental work is essential:

Fleeman, J. D., *A Bibliography of the Works of Samuel Johnson, Treating his published works from the beginnings to 1984*, 2 vols. (Oxford: Clarendon Press, 2000).

For secondary works, three complementary bibliographies should be consulted:

Clifford, James L., and Donald J. Greene, *Samuel Johnson: A Survey and Bibliography of Critical Studies* (Minneapolis: University of Minnesota Press, 1970).

Greene, Donald J., and John A. Vance, *A Bibliography of John-sonian Studies, 1970–1985* (Victoria: University of Victoria, 1987).

Lynch, Jack, *A Bibliography of Johnsonian Studies, 1986–1998* (New York: AMS Press, 2000).

There is also an online bibliography, compiled, maintained and updated by Jack Lynch at: http://andromeda.rutgers.edu/~jlynch/Johnson/sjbib.html

ON ORIENTAL TALES

Good starting points for further exploration of the oriental genre in Britain are three collections of tales, each with an informative introduction and apparatus:

Ballaster, Ros (ed.), *Fables of the East: Selected Tales, 1662–1785* (Oxford: Oxord University Press, 2005)

Mack, Robert L. (ed.), *Oriental Tales* (Oxford and New York: Oxford University Press, 1992).

Richardson, Alan (ed.), *Three Oriental Tales* (Boston and New York: Houghton Mifflin, 2002).

For criticism see:

Ballaster, Ros, *Fabulous Orients: Fictions of the East in England, 1662–1785* (Oxford: Oxford University Press, 2005). An up-to-date account of the narrative traffic between England and the Orient.

Conant, Martha P., *The Oriental Tale in England in the Eighteenth Century* (New York: Columbia University Press, 1908). Of its time but still interesting as a survey of the genre.

Porter, Roy, and G. S. Rousseau (eds.), *Exoticism in the Enlightenment* (Manchester: Manchester University Press, 1990).

Weitzman, Arthur, 'The Oriental Tale in the Eighteenth Century: A Reconsideration', *Studies on Voltaire in the Eighteenth Century*, 58 (1967), pp. 1839–55.

Note on the text

The first edition of *Rasselas* was published on 20 April 1759, printed by the firm of William Strahan for a group of book-sellers comprised of William Johnston and Robert and James Dodsley. It appeared in two octavo volumes, without Johnson's name, under the title *The Prince of Abissinia: A Tale* and it had a print run of 1,500 copies. A second edition was published on 26 June 1759 with light revisions that were almost certainly made by Johnson himself. Strahan's firm printed a total of six editions before Johnson's death in 1784; only the second shows signs of authorial revision. No manuscript of the work is known to survive.

The present text is based on a copy of the first edition held in the British Library (shelfmark: C.71.h.18). Johnson's revisions for the second edition have been incorporated, and the readings of the copy-text recorded below. Each of the original volumes is prefaced by its own contents list; the two lists have been combined here. The first page of the contents list for Vol. II of the first edition exists in two different states, with 'CONTENTS. / VOL. II' in the earlier state changed to 'CON-TENTS / OF THE SECOND VOLUME', so as to match the corresponding title in Volume I; the earlier state found in the copy-text has been emended here. A misnumbering of chapters – from Chapter XXIX onwards, both in the contents list and in the body of the text – has been corrected with the changes not recorded. Full stops after chapter numbers in the contents and after chapter numbers and titles in the text have been dropped. The first word in each chapter was all in capitals, but in this edition is upper and lower case.

Penguin housestyling has been applied to quotation marks (doubles have become singles, with doubles inside where appropriate); internal quotation marks have been added to interrupted speech (e.g. 'Ye, said he, are happy . . .' becomes 'Ye,' said he, 'are happy . . .'), and omitted opening or closing quotation marks have been supplied. The long 's' has been modernized.

The following emendations of proper names are applied throughout and not recorded: 'happy valley' and '*happy valley*' become 'Happy Valley', and 'red sea' becomes 'Red Sea'. A small number of mid-sentence capitals have been lower cased, with the changes recorded below.

Johnson's spelling has been retained even where it may seem strange to a modern reader (e.g. 'persue', 'emperour', 'publick', 'recal', 'carelesness', 'ransome'). When the spelling of a word varies in the first edition (e.g. 'ancient' and 'antient'; 'enforcement' and 'inforcement'; 'condemn' and 'contemn'), majority usage is followed; in the few cases where there is no clear majority, the modern spelling is adopted. All emendations to spelling are recorded below. (An oblique stroke indicates a line ending in the first edition that affected the text reading. The long 's' has been modernized.)

Page: line number	Penguin	1st edition
7:4	persue	pursue
7:9	father	Father
10:32	sages	Sages
16:5	passed	past
17:7	chearfully	cheerfully
22:18	enquire	inquire
22:18	enquiries	inquiries
24:12	negotiate	negociate
25:26	enquiries	inquiries
27:18	poetry	Poetry
27:20	angelick nature	Angelick Nature

27:28	nature and passion	Nature and Passion
28:16	desarts	deserts
28:27	enforcement	inforcement
29:23	condemn	contemn
31:18	journeys	journies
33:22	barbarians	Barbarians
35:1	enquiring	inquiring
40:30	wherever	where-/ever
42:35	gaiety	gay-/ety
48:2	glimpse	Glimpse
48:16	shepherds'	shepherds
54:22	that	That
58:6	summerhouse	summer-/house
60:1	practise	practice
63:17	querulous	querelous
64:32	falsehood	falshood
69:36	enquire	inquire
71:2	pyramids	Pyramids
71:14	shewed	showed
72:29	cowardice	cowardise
73:2	pyramid	Pyramid
73:12	barbarians	Barbarians
75:32	Governours	Governors
77:11	entreated	intreated
77:27	tranquility	tranquillity
82:10	monastery	monastry
82:11	desarts	deserts
82:16	monastery	monastry
83:29	persuits	pursuits
84:31	shew	show
89:36	despatch	dispatch
102:36	entreated	intreated
105:23	enters,	enters
107:37	persuits	pursuits
111:6	shewn	shown
111:15	ancient	antient
112:6	she	She

The following list gives Johnson's revisions to the 2nd edition (included in the Penguin text) and the 1st edition readings. (The ellipsis indicates omitted words in a long revision.)

Page: line number	2nd edition	1st edition
7:10	pours	powers
7:13	Rasselas	he
8:31	blissful	blisful
9:7	joined by	joined with
9:18	a long . . . had	successive monarchs
10:24	officiousness	endeavours
12:29	procure or purchase	procure
15:27	yet	but
18:22	having	and having
18:37	swimming	swiming
19:27	therefore	and
20:18	many	the
21:25	rehearsed	recited
23:2	losing them	losing
25:16	thought	hope
25:33	prince. Is	prince, is
26:5	warning,	warning you,
26:9	grieved to think	thought
27:27	whether, as	whether
27:28	same,	same, and
29:26	future	successive
29:27	place. [paragraph] "His	place. His
30:6	Proceed	Proceed now
31:23	fields	places
35:9	by	with the
35:37	heart.	heart, that
38:9	work	labour
38:23	toil	labour
38:30	long	often
42:5	favourite Pekuah	favourite
46:22	patience;	patienc;

51:37	preferments	preferment
51:38	feeling that . . . was	finding my vigour
52:18	exercise	practice
53:3	RASSELAS	RASSSELAS
53:29	said	says
56:16	think that	think
56:22	who	that
58:19	fury	fiend
65:2	alternately . . . and	affected by one or
65:15	. institution; will	institution. Will
68:29	them.	them. His look was clouded with thought.
69:18	require attention, and	necessarily require attention, and sufficiently
70:9	and the	and all the
71:29	in	up
74:5	perpetual	successive
77:22	languishes for want of	continues to lament
77:32	treasured	treasured up
79:12	communicated: they . . . them?	communicated.
80:19	remembered. The . . . sorrow.	remembered by the princess.
82:5	Rover	Arab
82:11	Anthony	Antony
82:23	receiving the . . . respect	he received the stipulated price, and, with great respect, restored her
83:20	on	up to
84:12	suppose	supposed
84:23	me.	me:
85:7	learn reverence or pity	have learned to spare
87:4	after your . . . weeks	a few weeks after your journey
87:10	on the richest couch	in the place of honour
87:22	are	were
88:29	receive solace from	be much solaced by
89:4	listen	listen long

92:10	great princess	Madam
92:17	quickly	always
92:22	often	sometimes
93:29	opinion of . . . justified	astronomer justifies his account of himself
109:19	mind	the mind
111:4	unperishable,	unperishable in itself,
111:4	superiour	higher
111:5	cause of decay,	cause
111:6	shown by	collected from

Quasi-facsimile transcription of the title-page of the first edition (1859)

THE
PRINCE
OF
ABISSINIA.

A

TALE.

IN TWO VOLUMES.

VOL. I.

LONDON:
Printed for R. and J. DODSLEY, in Pall-Mall;
and W. JOHNSTON, in Ludgate-Street.

MDCCLIX.

CONTENTS

OF THE

FIRST VOLUME.

CONTENTS

OF THE

SECOND VOLUME.

CHAP. I

Description of a palace in a valley

Ye who listen with credulity to the whispers of fancy, and persue with eagerness the phantoms of hope; who expect that age will perform the promises of youth, and that the deficiencies of the present day will be supplied by the morrow; attend to the history of Rasselas prince of Abissinia.[1]

Rasselas was the fourth son of the mighty emperour, in whose dominions the father of waters[2] begins his course; whose bounty pours down the streams of plenty, and scatters over half the world the harvests of Egypt.

According to the custom which has descended from age to age among the monarchs of the torrid zone, Rasselas was confined in a private palace, with the other sons and daughters of Abissinian royalty, till the order of succession should call him to the throne.

The place, which the wisdom or policy of antiquity had destined for the residence of the Abissinian princes, was a spacious valley in the kingdom of Amhara,[3] surrounded on every side by mountains, of which the summits overhang the middle part.[4] The only passage, by which it could be entered, was a cavern that passed under a rock, of which it has long been disputed whether it was the work of nature or of human industry. The outlet of the cavern was concealed by a thick wood, and the mouth which opened into the valley was closed with gates of iron, forged by the artificers of ancient days, so massy[5] that no man could, without the help of engines,[6] open or shut them.

From the mountains on every side, rivulets descended that filled all the valley with verdure and fertility, and formed a lake in the middle inhabited by fish of every species, and frequented by every fowl whom nature has taught to dip the wing in water. This lake discharged its superfluities by a stream which entered a dark cleft of the mountain on the northern side, and fell with dreadful noise from precipice to precipice till it was heard no more.

The sides of the mountains were covered with trees, the banks of the brooks were diversified with flowers; every blast shook spices from the rocks, and every month dropped fruits upon the ground. All animals that bite the grass, or brouse the shrub, whether wild or tame, wandered in this extensive circuit, secured from beasts of prey by the mountains which confined them. On one part were flocks and herds feeding in the pastures, on another all the beasts of chase frisking in the lawns; the spritely kid was bounding on the rocks, the subtle monkey frolicking in the trees, and the solemn elephant[7] reposing in the shade. All the diversities of the world were brought together, the blessings of nature were collected, and its evils extracted and excluded.

The valley, wide and fruitful, supplied its inhabitants with the necessaries of life, and all delights and superfluities were added at the annual visit which the emperour paid his children, when the iron gate was opened to the sound of musick; and during eight days every one that resided in the valley was required to propose whatever might contribute to make seclusion pleasant, to fill up the vacancies of attention, and lessen the tediousness of time. Every desire was immediately granted. All the artificers of pleasure were called to gladden the festivity; the musicians exerted the power of harmony, and the dancers shewed their activity before the princes, in hope that they should pass their lives in this blissful captivity, to which these only were admitted whose performance was thought able to add novelty to luxury. Such was the appearance of security and delight which this retirement afforded, that they to whom it was new always desired that it might be perpetual; and as those, on whom the iron gate had once closed, were never suffered to return, the effect of longer experience could not be known.

Thus every year produced new schemes of delight, and new competitors for imprisonment.

The palace stood on an eminence raised about thirty paces[8] above the surface of the lake. It was divided into many squares or courts, built with greater or less magnificence according to the rank of those for whom they were designed. The roofs were turned into arches of massy stone joined by a cement that grew harder by time, and the building stood from century to century, deriding the solstitial rains and equinoctial hurricanes, without need of reparation.

This house, which was so large as to be fully known to none but some ancient officers who successively inherited the secrets of the place, was built as if suspicion herself had dictated the plan. To every room there was an open and secret passage, every square had a communication with the rest, either from the upper stories by private galleries, or by subterranean passages from the lower apartments. Many of the columns had unsuspected cavities, in which a long race of monarchs had reposited their treasures. They then closed up the opening with marble, which was never to be removed but in the utmost exigencies of the kingdom; and recorded their accumulations in a book which was itself concealed in a tower not entered but by the emperour, attended by the prince who stood next in succession.

CHAP. II

The discontent of Rasselas in the Happy Valley

Here the sons and daughters of Abissinia[1] lived only to know the soft vicissitudes of pleasure and repose, attended by all that were skilful to delight, and gratified with whatever the senses can enjoy. They wandered in gardens of fragrance, and slept in the fortresses of security. Every art was practised to make them pleased with their own condition. The sages who instructed them, told them of nothing but the miseries of publick life, and described all beyond the mountains as regions of calamity, where discord was always raging, and where man preyed upon man.

To heighten their opinion of their own felicity, they were daily entertained with songs, the subject of which was the Happy Valley. Their appetites were excited by frequent enumerations of different enjoyments, and revelry and merriment was the business of every hour from the dawn of morning to the close of even.

These methods were generally successful; few of the princes had ever wished to enlarge their bounds, but passed their lives in full conviction that they had all within their reach that art or nature could bestow, and pitied those whom fate had excluded from this seat of tranquility, as the sport of chance, and the slaves of misery.

Thus they rose in the morning, and lay down at night, pleased with each other and with themselves, all but Rasselas, who, in the twenty-sixth year of his age, began to withdraw himself from their pastimes and assemblies, and to delight in solitary walks and silent meditation. He often sat before tables covered with luxury,[2] and forgot to taste the dainties that were placed before him: he rose abruptly in the midst of the song, and hastily retired beyond the sound of musick. His attendants observed the change and endeavoured to renew his love of pleasure: he neglected their officiousness,[3] repulsed their invitations, and spent day after day on the banks of rivulets sheltered with trees, where he sometimes listened to the birds in the branches, sometimes observed the fish playing in the stream, and anon[4] cast his eyes upon the pastures and mountains filled with animals, of which some were biting the herbage, and some sleeping among the bushes.

This singularity of his humour[5] made him much observed. One of the sages, in whose conversation he had formerly delighted, followed him secretly, in hope of discovering the cause of his disquiet. Rasselas, who knew not that any one was near him, having for some time fixed his eyes upon the goats that were brousing among the rocks, began to compare their condition with his own.

'What,' said he, 'makes the difference between man and all

the rest of the animal creation?[6] Every beast that strays beside me has the same corporal necessities with myself; he is hungry and crops the grass, he is thirsty and drinks the stream, his thirst and hunger are appeased, he is satisfied and sleeps; he rises again and is hungry, he is again fed and is at rest. I am hungry and thirsty like him, but when thirst and hunger cease I am not at rest; I am, like him, pained with want, but am not, like him, satisfied with fulness. The intermediate hours are tedious and gloomy; I long again to be hungry that I may again quicken my attention. The birds peck the berries or the corn, and fly away to the groves where they sit in seeming happiness on the branches, and waste their lives in tuning one unvaried series of sounds. I likewise can call the lutanist and the singer, but the sounds that pleased me yesterday weary me to day, and will grow yet more wearisome to morrow. I can discover within me no power of perception which is not glutted with its proper pleasure, yet I do not feel myself delighted. Man has surely some latent sense for which this place affords no gratification, or he has some desires distinct from sense which must be satisfied before he can be happy.'

After this he lifted up his head, and seeing the moon rising, walked towards the palace. As he passed through the fields, and saw the animals around him, 'Ye,' said he, 'are happy, and need not envy me that walk thus among you, burthened with myself; nor do I, ye gentle beings, envy your felicity; for it is not the felicity of man. I have many distresses from which ye are free; I fear pain when I do not feel it; I sometimes shrink at evils recollected, and sometimes start at evils anticipated: surely the equity of providence has ballanced peculiar sufferings with peculiar enjoyments.'

With observations like these the prince amused himself as he returned, uttering them with a plaintive voice, yet with a look that discovered[7] him to feel some complacence in his own perspicacity, and to receive some solace of the miseries of life, from consciousness of the delicacy with which he felt, and the eloquence with which he bewailed them. He mingled cheerfully in the diversions of the evening, and all rejoiced to find that his heart was lightened.

CHAP. III

The wants of him that wants nothing

On the next day his old instructor, imagining that he had now made himself acquainted with his disease of mind, was in hope of curing it by counsel, and officiously sought an opportunity of conference, which the prince, having long considered him as one whose intellects were exhausted, was not very willing to afford: 'Why,' said he, 'does this man thus intrude upon me; shall I be never suffered to forget those lectures which pleased only while they were new, and to become new again must be forgotten?' He then walked into the wood, and composed himself to his usual meditations; when, before his thoughts had taken any settled form, he perceived his persuer at his side, and was at first prompted by his impatience to go hastily away; but, being unwilling to offend a man whom he had once reverenced and still loved, he invited him to sit down with him on the bank.

The old man, thus encouraged, began to lament the change which had been lately observed in the prince, and to enquire why he so often retired from the pleasures of the palace, to loneliness and silence. 'I fly from pleasure,' said the prince, 'because pleasure has ceased to please; I am lonely because I am miserable, and am unwilling to cloud with my presence the happiness of others.' 'You, Sir,' said the sage, 'are the first who has complained of misery in the Happy Valley. I hope to convince you that your complaints have no real cause. You are here in full possession of all that the emperour of Abissinia can bestow; here is neither labour to be endured nor danger to be dreaded, yet here is all that labour or danger can procure or purchase. Look round and tell me which of your wants is without supply: if you want nothing, how are you unhappy?'

'That I want nothing,' said the prince, 'or that I know not what I want, is the cause of my complaint; if I had any known want, I should have a certain wish; that wish would excite endeavour, and I should not then repine to see the sun move so slowly towards the western mountain, or lament when breaks and sleep will no longer hide me from myself. I see the kids and the lambs chasing one another, I fancy should be happy if I had something to persue. But, posse ...g all that I can want, I find one day and one hour exactly like another, except that the latter is still more tedious than the former. Let your experience inform me how the day may now seem as short as in my childhood, while nature was yet fresh, and every moment shewed me what I never had observed before. I have already enjoyed too much; give me something to desire.'

The old man was surprised at this new species of affliction, and knew not what to reply, yet was unwilling to be silent. 'Sir,' said he, 'if you had seen the miseries of the world, you would know how to value your present state.' 'Now,' said the prince, 'you have given me something to desire; I shall long to see the miseries of the world, since the sight of them is necessary to happiness.'[1]

CHAP. IV

The prince continues to grieve and muse

At this time the sound of musick proclaimed the hour of repast, and the conversation was concluded. The old man went away sufficiently discontented to find that his reasonings had produced the only conclusion which they were intended to prevent. But in the decline of life shame and grief are of short duration; whether it be that we bear easily what we have born long, or that, finding ourselves in age less regarded, we less regard others; or, that we look with slight regard upon afflictions, to which we know that the hand of death is about to put an end.

The prince, whose views were extended to a wider space, could not speedily quiet his emotions. He had been before terrified at the length of life which nature promised him, because he considered that in a long time much must be endured; he now rejoiced in his youth, because in many years much might be done.

This first beam of hope, that had been ever darted into his mind, rekindled youth in his cheeks, and doubled the lustre of his eyes.[1] He was fired with the desire of doing something, though he knew not yet with distinctness, either end or means.

He was now no longer gloomy and unsocial; but, considering himself as master of a secret stock of happiness, which he could enjoy only by concealing it, he affected to be busy in all schemes of diversion, and endeavoured to make others pleased with the state of which he himself was weary. But pleasures never can be so multiplied or continued, as not to leave much of life unemployed; there were many hours, both of the night and day, which he could spend without suspicion in solitary thought. The load of life was much lightened: he went eagerly into the assemblies, because he supposed the frequency of his presence necessary to the success of his purposes; he retired gladly to privacy, because he had now a subject of thought.

His chief amusement was to picture to himself that world which he had never seen; to place himself in various conditions; to be entangled in imaginary difficulties, and to be engaged in wild adventures: but his benevolence always terminated his projects in the relief of distress, the detection of fraud, the defeat of oppression, and the diffusion of happiness.

Thus passed twenty months of the life of Rasselas. He busied himself so intensely in visionary bustle, that he forgot his real solitude; and, amidst hourly preparations for the various incidents of human affairs, neglected to consider by what means he should mingle with mankind.

One day, as he was sitting on a bank, he feigned to himself an orphan virgin robbed of her little portion[2] by a treacherous lover, and crying after him for restitution and redress. So strongly was the image impressed upon his mind, that he started up in the maid's defence, and run[3] forward to seize the plunderer with all the eagerness of real persuit. Fear naturally quickens the flight of guilt. Rasselas could not catch the fugitive with his utmost efforts; but, resolving to weary, by perseverance, him

whom he could not surpass in speed, he pressed on till the
of the mountain stopped his course.

Here he recollected himself, and smiled at his own usele
impetuosity. Then raising his eyes to the mountain, 'This,' said
he, 'is the fatal[4] obstacle that hinders at once the enjoyment of
pleasure, and the exercise of virtue. How long is it that my
hopes and wishes have flown beyond this boundary of my life,
which yet I never have attempted to surmount!'

Struck with this reflection, he sat down to muse, and
remembered, that since he first resolved to escape from his
confinement, the sun had passed twice over him in his annual
course. He now felt a degree of regret with which he had never
been before acquainted. He considered how much might have
been done in the time which had passed, and left nothing real
behind it.[5] He compared twenty months with the life of man.
'In life,' said he, 'is not to be counted the ignorance of infancy,
or imbecility of age. We are long before we are able to think,
and we soon cease from the power of acting. The true period
of human existence may be reasonably estimated as forty years,
of which I have mused away the four and twentieth part. What
I have lost was certain, for I have certainly possessed it; but of
twenty months to come who can assure me?'

The consciousness of his own folly pierced him deeply, and
he was long before he could be reconciled to himself. 'The rest
of my time,' said he, 'has been lost by the crime or folly of my
ancestors, and the absurd institutions of my country; I remember it with disgust, yet without remorse: but the months that
have passed since new light darted into my soul, since I formed
a scheme of reasonable felicity, have been squandered by my
own fault. I have lost that which can never be restored: I have
seen the sun rise and set for twenty months, an idle gazer on
the light of heaven: In this time the birds have left the nest of
their mother, and committed themselves to the woods and to
the skies: the kid has forsaken the teat, and learned by degrees
to climb the rocks in quest of independant sustenance. I only
have made no advances, but am still helpless and ignorant. The
moon, by more than twenty changes, admonished me of the

flux of life; the stream that rolled before my feet upbraided my inactivity. I sat feasting on intellectual luxury, regardless alike of the examples of the earth, and the instructions of the planets. Twenty months are past, who shall restore them!'

These sorrowful meditations fastened upon his mind; he passed four months in resolving to lose no more time in idle resolves[6] and was awakened to more vigorous exertion by hearing a maid, who had broken a porcelain cup, remark, that what cannot be repaired is not to be regretted.

This was obvious; and Rasselas reproached himself that he had not discovered it, having not known, or not considered, how many useful hints are obtained by chance, and how often the mind, hurried by her own ardour to distant views, neglects the truths that lie open before her. He, for a few hours, regretted his regret, and from that time bent his whole mind upon the means of escaping from the valley of happiness.

CHAP. V

The prince meditates his escape

He now found that it would be very difficult to effect that which it was very easy to suppose effected. When he looked round about him, he saw himself confined by the bars of nature which had never yet been broken, and by the gate, through which none that once had passed it were ever able to return.[1] He was now impatient as an eagle in a grate.[2] He passed week after week in clambering the mountains, to see if there was any aperture which the bushes might conceal, but found all the summits inaccessible by their prominence.[3] The iron gate he despaired to open; for it was not only secured with all the power of art, but was always watched by successive sentinels, and was by its position exposed to the perpetual observation of all the inhabitants.

He then examined the cavern through which the waters of the lake were discharged; and, looking down at a time when the sun shone strongly upon its mouth, he discovered it to be full of broken rocks, which, though they permitted the stream to flow through many narrow passages, would stop any body of solid bulk. He returned discouraged and dejected; but, having now known the blessing of hope, resolved never to despair.

In these fruitless searches he spent ten months. The time, however, passed chearfully away: in the morning he rose with new hope, in the evening applauded his own diligence, and in the night slept sound after his fatigue. He met a thousand amusements which beguiled his labour, and diversified his thoughts. He discerned the various instincts of animals, and properties of plants, and found the place replete with wonders, of which he purposed to solace himself with the contemplation, if he should never be able to accomplish his flight; rejoicing that his endeavours, though yet unsuccessful, had supplied him with a source of inexhaustible enquiry.

But his original curiosity was not yet abated; he resolved to obtain some knowledge of the ways of men. His wish still continued, but his hope grew less. He ceased to survey any longer the walls of his prison, and spared to search by new toils for interstices which he knew could not be found, yet determined to keep his design always in view, and lay hold on any expedient that time should offer.

CHAP. VI

A dissertation on the art of flying[1]

Among the artists[2] that had been allured into the Happy Valley, to labour for the accommodation and pleasure of its inhabitants, was a man eminent for his knowledge of the mechanick powers, who had contrived many engines both of use and recreation. By a wheel, which the stream turned, he forced the water into a tower, whence it was distributed to all the apartments of the palace. He erected a pavillion in the garden, around which he kept the air always cool by artificial showers.

One of the groves, appropriated to the ladies, was ventilated by fans, to which the rivulet that run through it gave a constant motion; and instruments of soft musick were placed at proper distances, of which some played by the impulse of the wind, and some by the power of the stream.

This artist was sometimes visited by Rasselas, who was pleased with every kind of knowledge, imagining that the time would come when all his acquisitions should be of use to him in the open world. He came one day to amuse himself in his usual manner, and found the master busy in building a sailing chariot: he saw that the design was practicable upon a level surface, and with expressions of great esteem solicited its completion. The workman was pleased to find himself so much regarded by the prince, and resolved to gain yet higher honours. 'Sir,' said he, 'you have seen but a small part of what the mechanick sciences can perform. I have been long of opinion, that, instead of the tardy conveyance of ships and chariots, man might use the swifter migration of wings; that the fields of air are open to knowledge, and that only ignorance and idleness need crawl upon the ground.'

This hint rekindled the prince's desire of passing the mountains; having seen what the mechanist had already performed, he was willing to fancy that he could do more; yet resolved to enquire further before he suffered hope to afflict him by disappointment. 'I am afraid,' said he to the artist, 'that your imagination prevails over your skill, and that you now tell me rather what you wish than what you know. Every animal has his element assigned him; the birds have the air, and man and beasts the earth.' 'So,' replied the mechanist, 'fishes have the water, in which yet beasts can swim by nature, and men by art. He that can swim needs not despair to fly: to swim is to fly in a grosser fluid, and to fly is to swim in a subtler.[3] We are only to proportion our power of resistance to the different density of the matter through which we are to pass. You will be necessarily upborn by the air, if you can renew any impulse upon it, faster than the air can recede from the pressure.'

'But the exercise of swimming,' said the prince, 'is very laborious; the strongest limbs are soon wearied; I am afraid the act of flying will be yet more violent, and wings will be of no great use, unless we can fly further than we can swim.'

'The labour of rising from the ground,' said the artist, 'will be great, as we see it in the heavier domestick fowls; but, as we mount higher, the earth's attraction, and the body's gravity, will be gradually diminished, till we shall arrive at a region where the man will float in the air without any tendency to fall: no care will then be necessary, but to move forwards, which the gentlest impulse will effect. You, Sir, whose curiosity is so extensive, will easily conceive with what pleasure a philosopher, furnished with wings, and hovering in the sky, would see the earth, and all its inhabitants, rolling beneath him, and presenting to him successively, by its diurnal motion, all the countries within the same parallel.[4] How must it amuse the pendent spectator to see the moving scene of land and ocean, cities and desarts! To survey with equal security the marts of trade, and the fields of battle; mountains infested by barbarians, and fruitful regions gladdened by plenty, and lulled by peace! How easily shall we then trace the Nile through all his passage; pass over to distant regions, and examine the face of nature from one extremity of the earth to the other!'

'All this,' said the prince, 'is much to be desired, but I am afraid that no man will be able to breathe in these regions of speculation[5] and tranquility. I have been told, that respiration is difficult upon lofty mountains, yet from these precipices, though so high as to produce great tenuity of the air, it is very easy to fall: therefore I suspect, that from any height, where life can be supported, there may be danger of too quick descent.'

'Nothing,' replied the artist, 'will ever be attempted, if all possible objections must be first overcome. If you will favour my project I will try the first flight at my own hazard. I have considered the structure of all volant[6] animals, and find the folding continuity of the bat's wings most easily accommodated to the human form. Upon this model I shall begin my task to morrow, and in a year expect to tower into the air beyond the malice or pursuit of man. But I will work only on this condition, that the art shall not be divulged, and that you shall not require me to make wings for any but ourselves.'

'Why,' said Rasselas, 'should you envy others so great an advantage? All skill ought to be exerted for universal good; every man has owed much to others, and ought to repay the kindness that he has received.'[7]

'If men were all virtuous,' returned the artist, 'I should with great alacrity teach them all to fly. But what would be the security of the good, if the bad could at pleasure invade them from the sky? Against an army sailing through the clouds neither walls, nor mountains, nor seas, could afford any security. A flight of northern savages might hover in the wind, and light at once with irresistible violence upon the capital of a fruitful region that was rolling under them.[8] Even this valley, the retreat of princes, the abode of happiness, might be violated by the sudden descent of some of the naked nations that swarm on the coast of the southern sea.'

The prince promised secrecy, and waited for the performance, not wholly hopeless of success. He visited the work from time to time, observed its progress, and remarked many ingenious contrivances to facilitate motion, and unite levity with strength. The artist was every day more certain that he should leave vultures and eagles behind him, and the contagion of his confidence seized upon the prince.

In a year the wings were finished, and, on a morning appointed, the maker appeared furnished for flight on a little promontory: he waved his pinions a while to gather air, then leaped from his stand, and in an instant dropped into the lake. His wings, which were of no use in the air, sustained him in the water, and the prince drew him to land, half dead with terrour and vexation.

CHAP. VII

The prince finds a man of learning

The prince was not much afflicted by this disaster, having suffered himself to hope for a happier event, only because he had no other means of escape in view. He still persisted in his design to leave the Happy Valley by the first opportunity.

His imagination was now at a stand; he had no prospect of entering into the world; and, notwithstanding all his endeavours to support[1] himself, discontent by degrees preyed upon him, and he began again to lose his thoughts in sadness, when the rainy season, which in these countries is periodical, made it inconvenient to wander in the woods.

The rain continued longer and with more violence than had been ever known: the clouds broke on the surrounding mountains, and the torrents streamed into the plain on every side, till the cavern was too narrow to discharge the water. The lake overflowed its banks, and all the level of the valley was covered with the inundation. The eminence, on which the palace was built, and some other spots of rising ground, were all that the eye could now discover. The herds and flocks left the pastures, and both the wild beasts and the tame retreated to the mountains.

This inundation confined all the princes to domestick amusements, and the attention of Rasselas was particularly seized by a poem, which Imlac[2] rehearsed,[3] upon the various conditions of humanity. He commanded the poet to attend him in his apartment, and recite his verses a second time; then entering into familiar talk, he thought himself happy in having found a man who knew the world so well, and could so skilfully paint the scenes of life. He asked a thousand questions about things, to which, though common to all other mortals, his confinement from childhood had kept him a stranger. The poet pitied his ignorance, and loved his curiosity, and entertained him from day to day with novelty and instruction, so that the prince regretted the necessity of sleep, and longed till the morning should renew his pleasure.

As they were sitting together, the prince commanded Imlac to relate his history, and to tell by what accident he was forced, or by what motive induced, to close his life in the Happy Valley. As he was going to begin his narrative, Rasselas was called to a concert, and obliged to restrain his curiosity till the evening.

CHAP. VIII

The history of Imlac

The close of the day is, in the regions of the torrid zone, the only season of diversion and entertainment, and it was therefore mid-night before the musick ceased, and the princesses retired. Rasselas then called for his companion and required him to begin the story of his life.

'Sir,' said Imlac, 'my history will not be long: the life that is devoted to knowledge passes silently away, and is very little diversified by events. To talk in publick, to think in solitude, to read and to hear, to enquire, and answer enquiries, is the business of a scholar.[1] He wanders about the world without pomp or terrour,[2] and is neither known nor valued but by men like himself.

'I was born in the kingdom of Goiama,[3] at no great distance from the fountain of the Nile. My father was a wealthy merchant, who traded between the inland countries of Africk and the ports of the Red Sea. He was honest, frugal and diligent, but of mean sentiments, and narrow comprehension: he desired only to be rich, and to conceal his riches, lest he should be spoiled[4] by the governours of the province.'[5]

'Surely,' said the prince, 'my father must be negligent of his charge, if any man in his dominions dares take that which belongs to another. Does he not know that kings are accountable for injustice permitted as well as done? If I were emperour, not the meanest of my subjects should be oppressed with impunity. My blood boils when I am told that a merchant durst not enjoy his honest gains for fear of losing them by the rapacity of power. Name the governour who robbed the people, that I may declare his crimes to the emperour.'

'Sir,' said Imlac, 'your ardour is the natural effect of virtue animated by youth: the time will come when you will acquit your father, and perhaps hear with less impatience of the governour. Oppression is, in the Abissinian dominions, neither frequent nor tolerated; but no form of government has been yet discovered, by which cruelty can be wholly prevented. Subordination supposes power on one part and subjection on the other; and if power be in the hands of men, it will sometimes be abused. The vigilance of the supreme magistrate may do much, but much will still remain undone. He can never know all the crimes that are committed, and can seldom punish all that he knows.'

'This,' said the prince, 'I do not understand, but I had rather hear thee than dispute. Continue thy narration.'

'My father,' proceeded Imlac, 'originally intended that I should have no other education, than such as might qualify me for commerce; and discovering in me great strength of memory, and quickness of apprehension, often declared his hope that I should be some time the richest man in Abissinia.'

'Why,' said the prince, 'did thy father desire the increase of his wealth, when it was already greater than he durst discover or enjoy? I am unwilling to doubt thy veracity, yet inconsistencies cannot both be true.'

'Inconsistencies,' answered Imlac, 'cannot both be right, but, imputed to man, they may both be true. Yet diversity is not inconsistency. My father might expect a time of greater security. However, some desire is necessary to keep life in motion, and he, whose real wants are supplied, must admit those of fancy.'

'This,' said the prince, 'I can in some measure conceive. I repent that I interrupted thee.'

'With this hope,' proceeded Imlac, 'he sent me to school; but when I had once found the delight of knowledge, and felt the pleasure of intelligence and the pride of invention, I began silently to despise riches, and determined to disappoint the purpose of my father, whose grossness of conception raised my pity. I was twenty years old before his tenderness would expose me to the fatigue of travel, in which time I had been instructed, by successive masters, in all the literature[6] of my native country. As every hour taught me something new, I lived in a continual course of gratifications; but, as I advanced towards manhood, I lost much of the reverence with which I had been used to look on my instructors; because, when the lesson was ended, I did not find them wiser or better than common men.

'At length my father resolved to initiate me in commerce, and, opening one of his subterranean treasuries, counted out ten thousand pieces of gold. "This, young man," said he, "is the stock with which you must negotiate.[7] I began with less than the fifth part, and you see how diligence and parsimony have increased it. This is your own to waste or to improve. If you squander it by negligence or caprice, you must wait for my death before you will be rich: if, in four years, you double your stock, we will thenceforward let subordination cease, and live together as friends and partners; for he shall always be equal with me, who is equally skilled in the art of growing rich."

'We laid our money upon camels, concealed in bales of cheap goods, and travelled to the shore of the Red Sea. When I cast my eye on the expanse of waters my heart bounded like that of a prisoner escaped. I felt an unextinguishable curiosity kindle in my mind, and resolved to snatch this opportunity of seeing the manners of other nations, and of learning sciences[8] unknown in Abissinia.

'I remembered that my father had obliged me to the improvement of my stock, not by a promise which I ought not to violate, but by a penalty which I was at liberty to incur, and therefore determined to gratify my predominant desire, and by drinking at the fountains of knowledge, to quench the thirst of curiosity.

'As I was supposed to trade without connexion with my father, it was easy for me to become acquainted with the master of a ship, and procure a passage to some other country. I had no motives of choice to regulate my voyage; it was sufficient for me that, wherever I wandered, I should see a country which I had not seen before. I therefore entered a ship bound for Surat,[9] having left a letter for my father declaring my intention.

CHAP. IX

The history of Imlac continued

'When I first entered upon the world of waters, and lost sight of land, I looked round about me with pleasing terrour,[1] and thinking my soul enlarged by the boundless prospect, imagined that I could gaze round for ever without satiety; but, in a short time, I grew weary of looking on barren uniformity, where I could only see again what I had already seen. I then descended into the ship, and doubted for a while whether all my future pleasures would not end like this in disgust and disappointment. "Yet, surely," said I, "the ocean and the land are very different; the only variety of water is rest and motion, but the earth has mountains and vallies, desarts and cities: it is inhabited by men of different customs and contrary opinions; and I may hope to find variety in life, though I should miss it in nature."

'With this thought I quieted my mind, and amused myself during the voyage; sometimes by learning from the sailors the art of navigation, which I have never practised, and sometimes by forming schemes for my conduct in different situations, in not one of which I have been ever placed.

'I was almost weary of my naval amusements when we landed safely at Surat. I secured my money, and purchasing some commodities for show, joined myself to a caravan that was passing into the inland country. My companions, for some reason or other, conjecturing that I was rich, and, by my enquiries and admiration,[2] finding that I was ignorant, considered me as a novice whom they had a right to cheat, and who was to learn at the usual expence the art of fraud. They exposed me to the theft of servants, and the exaction of officers, and saw me plundered upon false pretences, without any advantage to themselves, but that of rejoicing in the superiority of their own knowledge.'

'Stop a moment,' said the prince. 'Is there such depravity in man, as that he should injure another without benefit to himself? I can easily conceive that all are pleased with superiority;

but your ignorance was merely accidental, which, being neither your crime nor your folly, could afford them no reason to applaud themselves; and the knowledge which they had, and which you wanted, they might as effectually have shewn by warning, as betraying you.'

'Pride,' said Imlac, 'is seldom delicate, it will please itself with very mean advantages; and envy feels not its own happiness, but when it may be compared with the misery of others. They were my enemies because they grieved to think me rich, and my oppressors because they delighted to find me weak.'

'Proceed,' said the prince: 'I doubt not of the facts which you relate, but imagine that you impute them to mistaken motives.'

'In this company,' said Imlac, 'I arrived at Agra, the capital of Indostan, the city in which the great Mogul[3] commonly resides. I applied myself to the language of the country, and in a few months was able to converse with the learned men; some of whom I found morose and reserved, and others easy and communicative; some were unwilling to teach another what they had with difficulty learned themselves; and some shewed that the end of their studies was to gain the dignity of instructing.

'To the tutor of the young princes I recommended myself so much, that I was presented to the emperour as a man of uncommon knowledge. The emperour asked me many questions concerning my country and my travels; and though I cannot now recollect any thing that he uttered above the power of a common man, he dismissed me astonished at his wisdom, and enamoured of his goodness.

'My credit was now so high, that the merchants, with whom I had travelled, applied to me for recommendations to the ladies of the court. I was surprised at their confidence of solicitation, and gently reproached them with their practices on the road. They heard me with cold indifference, and shewed no tokens of shame or sorrow.

'They then urged their request with the offer of a bribe; but what I would not do for kindness I would not do for money; and refused them, not because they had injured me, but because I would not enable them to injure others; for I knew they would have made use of my credit to cheat those who should buy their wares.

'Having resided at Agra, till there was no more to be learned, I travelled into Persia, where I saw many remains of ancient magnificence,[4] and observed many new accommodations[5] of life. The Persians are a nation eminently social,[6] and their assemblies afforded me daily opportunities of remarking characters and manners, and of tracing human nature through all its variations.

✳'From Persia I passed into Arabia, where I saw a nation at once pastoral and warlike;[7] who live without any settled habitation; whose only wealth is their flocks and herds; and who have yet carried on, through all ages, an hereditary war with all mankind, though they neither covet nor envy their possessions.

CHAP. X

Imlac's history continued. A dissertation upon poetry[1]

'Wherever I went, I found that poetry was considered as the highest learning, and regarded with a veneration somewhat approaching to that which man would pay to the angelick nature.[2] And it yet fills me with wonder, that, in almost all countries, the most ancient poets are considered as the best:[3] whether it be that every other kind of knowledge is an acquisition gradually attained, and poetry is a gift conferred at once; or that the first poetry of every nation surprised them as a novelty, and retained the credit by consent which it received by accident at first: or whether, as the province of poetry is to describe nature and passion, which are always the same,[4] the first writers took possession of the most striking objects for description, and the most probable occurrences for fiction, and left nothing to those that followed them, but transcription of the same events, and new combinations of the same images.

Whatever be the reason, it is commonly observed that the early writers are in possession of nature, and their followers of art: that the first excel in strength and invention, and the latter in elegance and refinement.[5]

'I was desirous to add my name to this illustrious fraternity. I read all the poets of Persia and Arabia, and was able to repeat by memory the volumes that are suspended in the mosque of Mecca.[6] But I soon found that no man was ever great by imitation. My desire of excellence impelled me to transfer my attention to nature and to life. Nature was to be my subject, and men to be my auditors: I could never describe what I had not seen: I could not hope to move those with delight or terrour, whose interests and opinions I did not understand.

'Being now resolved to be a poet, I saw every thing with a new purpose; my sphere of attention was suddenly magnified: no kind of knowledge was to be overlooked. I ranged mountains and desarts for images and resemblances, and pictured upon my mind every tree of the forest and flower of the valley. I observed with equal care the crags of the rock and the pinnacles of the palace. Sometimes I wandered along the mazes of the rivulet, and sometimes watched the changes of the summer clouds. To a poet nothing can be useless. Whatever is beautiful, and whatever is dreadful, must be familiar to his imagination: he must be conversant with all that is awfully vast or elegantly little. The plants of the garden, the animals of the wood, the minerals of the earth, and meteors of the sky, must all concur to store his mind with inexhaustible variety: for every idea[8] is useful for the enforcement or decoration of moral or religious truth; and he, who knows most, will have most power of diversifying his scenes, and of gratifying his reader with remote allusions and unexpected instruction.[9]

'All the appearances of nature I was therefore careful to study, and every country which I have surveyed has contributed something to my poetical powers.'

'In so wide a survey,' said the prince, 'you must surely have left much unobserved. I have lived, till now, within the circuit of these mountains, and yet cannot walk abroad without the sight of something which I had never 'seen before, or never heeded.'

'The business of a poet,' said Imlac, is to examine, not the individual, but the species; to remark general properties and large appearances: he does not number the streaks of the tulip, or describe the different shades in the verdure of the forest. He is to exhibit in his portraits of nature such prominent and striking features, as recal the original to every mind; and must neglect the minuter discriminations, which one may have remarked, and another have neglected, for those characteristicks which are alike obvious to vigilance and carelesness.[10]

'But the knowledge of nature is only half the task of a poet; he must be acquainted likewise with all the modes of life. His character requires that he estimate the happiness and misery of every condition; observe the power of all the passions in all their combinations, and trace the changes of the human mind as they are modified by various institutions and accidental influences of climate or custom, from the spriteliness of infancy to the despondence of decrepitude. He must divest himself of the prejudices of his age or country; he must consider right and wrong in their abstracted and invariable state; he must disregard present laws and opinions, and rise to general and transcendental truths, which will always be the same: he must therefore content himself with the slow progress of his name; condemn the applause of his own time, and commit his claims to the justice of posterity. He must write as the interpreter of nature, and the legislator of mankind, and consider himself as presiding over the thoughts and manners of future generations; as a being superiour to time and place.

'His labour is not yet at an end: he must know many languages and many sciences; and, that his stile may be worthy of his thoughts, must, by incessant practice, familiarize to himself every delicacy of speech and grace of harmony.'

CHAP. XI

Imlac's narrative continued. A hint on pilgrima

Imlac now felt the enthusiastic[1] fit, and was proceedi
aggrandize his own profession, when the prince cried
'Enough! Thou hast convinced me, that no human being
ever be a poet. Proceed with thy narration.'

'To be a poet,' said Imlac, 'is indeed very difficult.' 'So diffi
cult,' returned the prince, 'that I will at present hear no more
of his labours. Tell me whither you went when you had seen
Persia.'

'From Persia,' said the poet, 'I travelled through Syria, and
for three years resided in Palestine, where I conversed with
great numbers of the northern and western nations of Europe;
the nations which are now in possession of all power and
all knowledge; whose armies are irresistible, and whose fleets
command the remotest parts of the globe. When I compared
these men with the natives of our own kingdom, and those that
surround us, they appeared almost another order of beings. In
their countries it is difficult to wish for any thing that may not
be obtained: a thousand arts, of which we never heard, are
continually labouring for their convenience and pleasure; and
whatever their own climate has denied them is supplied by their
commerce.'

'By what means,' said the prince, 'are the Europeans thus
powerful? or why, since they can so easily visit Asia and Africa
for trade or conquest, cannot the Asiaticks and Africans invade
their coasts, plant colonies in their ports, and give laws to their
natural princes? The same wind that carries them back would
bring us thither.'

'They are more powerful, Sir, than we,' answered Imlac,
'because they are wiser; knowledge will always predominate
over ignorance, as man governs the other animals. But why
their knowledge is more than ours, I know not what reason can
be given, but the unsearchable will of the Supreme Being.'[2]

'When,' said the prince with a sigh, 'shall I be able to visit

Palestine, and mingle with this mighty confluence of nations?
Till that happy moment shall arrive, let me fill up the time with
such representations as thou canst give me. I am not ignorant
of the motive that assembles such numbers in that place, and
cannot but consider it as the center of wisdom and piety, to
which the best and wisest men of every land must be continually
resorting.'[3]

'There are some nations,' said Imlac, 'that send few visitants
to Palestine; for many numerous and learned sects in Europe,
concur to censure pilgrimage as superstitious, or deride it as
ridiculous.'

'You know,' said the prince, 'how little my life has made me
acquainted with diversity of opinions: it will be too long to
hear the arguments on both sides; you, that have considered
them, tell me the result.'

'Pilgrimage,' said Imlac, 'like many other acts of piety, may
be reasonable or superstitious, according to the principles upon
which it is performed. Long journeys in search of truth are not
commanded. Truth, such as is necessary to the regulation of
life, is always found where it is honestly sought. Change of
place is no natural cause of the increase of piety, for it inevitably
produces dissipation of mind. Yet, since men go every day to
view the fields where great actions have been performed, and
return with stronger impressions of the event, curiosity of the
same kind may naturally dispose us to view that country whence
our religion[4] had its beginning; and I believe no man surveys
those awful[5] scenes without some confirmation of holy reso-
lutions. That the Supreme Being may be more easily propitiated
in one place than in another, is the dream of idle superstition;
but that some places may operate upon our own minds in an
uncommon manner, is an opinion which hourly experience
will justify.[6] He who supposes that his vices may be more
successfully combated in Palestine, will, perhaps, find himself
mistaken, yet he may go thither without folly: he who thinks
they will be more freely pardoned, dishonours at once his reason
and religion.'

'These,' said the prince, 'are European distinctions. I will consider them another time. What have you found to be the effect of knowledge? Are those nations happier than we?'

'There is so much infelicity,' said the poet, 'in the world, that scarce any man has leisure from his own distresses to estimate the comparative happiness of others. Knowledge is certainly one of the means of pleasure, as is confessed by the natural desire which every mind feels of increasing its ideas.[7] Ignorance is mere privation, by which nothing can be produced: it is a vacuity in which the soul sits motionless and torpid for want of attraction; and, without knowing why, we always rejoice when we learn, and grieve when we forget. I am therefore inclined to conclude, that, if nothing counteracts the natural consequence of learning, we grow more happy as our minds take a wider range.

'In enumerating the particular comforts of life we shall find many advantages on the side of the Europeans. They cure wounds and diseases with which we languish and perish. We suffer inclemencies of weather which they can obviate. They have engines for the despatch of many laborious works, which we must perform by manual industry. There is such communication between distant places, that one friend can hardly be said to be absent from another. Their policy[8] removes all publick inconveniencies: they have roads cut through their mountains, and bridges laid upon their rivers. And, if we descend to the privacies of life, their habitations are more commodious, and their possessions are more secure.'

'They are surely happy,' said the prince, 'who have all these conveniencies, of which I envy none so much as the facility with which separated friends interchange their thoughts.'

'The Europeans,' answered Imlac, 'are less unhappy than we, but they are not happy. Human life is every where a state in which much is to be endured, and little to be enjoyed.'[9]

CHAP. XII

The story of Imlac continued

'I am not yet willing,' said the prince, 'to suppose that happiness is so parsimoniously distributed to mortals; nor can believe but that, if I had the choice of life,[1] I should be able to fill every day with pleasure. I would injure no man, and should provoke no resentment: I would relieve every distress, and should enjoy the benedictions of gratitude. I would choose my friends among the wise, and my wife among the virtuous; and therefore should be in no danger from treachery, or unkindness. My children should, by my care, be learned and pious, and would repay to my age what their childhood had received. What would dare to molest him who might call on every side to thousands enriched by his bounty, or assisted by his power? And why should not life glide quietly away in the soft reciprocation of protection and reverence? All this may be done without the help of European refinements, which appear by their effects to be rather specious than useful. Let us leave them and persue our journey.'

'From Palestine,' said Imlac, 'I passed through many regions of Asia; in the more civilized kingdoms as a trader, and among the barbarians of the mountains as a pilgrim. At last I began to long for my native country, that I might repose after my travels, and fatigues, in the places where I had spent my earliest years, and gladden my old companions with the recital of my adventures. Often did I figure to myself those, with whom I had sported away the gay hours of dawning life, sitting round me in its evening, wondering at my tales, and listening to my counsels.

'When this thought had taken possession of my mind, I considered every moment as wasted which did not bring me nearer to Abissinia. I hastened into Egypt, and, notwithstanding my impatience, was detained ten months in the contemplation of its ancient magnificence, and in enquiries after the remains of its ancient learning.[2] I found in Cairo a mixture of all nations;

some brought thither by the love of knowledge, some by the hope of gain, and many by the desire of living after their own manner without observation, and of lying hid in the obscurity of multitudes: for, in a city, populous as Cairo, it is possible to obtain at the same time the gratifications of society, and the secrecy of solitude.

'From Cairo I travelled to Suez,[3] and embarked on the Red Sea, passing along the coast till I arrived at the port from which I had departed twenty years before. Here I joined myself to a caravan and re-entered my native country.

'I now expected the caresses of my kinsmen, and the congratulations of my friends, and was not without hope that my father, whatever value he had set upon riches, would own with gladness and pride a son who was able to add to the felicity and honour of the nation. But I was soon convinced that my thoughts were vain. My father had been dead fourteen years, having divided his wealth among my brothers, who were removed to some other provinces. Of my companions the greater part was in the grave, of the rest some could with difficulty remember me, and some considered me as one corrupted by foreign manners.

'A man used to vicissitudes is not easily dejected. I forgot, after a time, my disappointment, and endeavoured to recommend myself to the nobles of the kingdom: they admitted me to their tables, heard my story, and dismissed me. I opened a school, and was prohibited to teach. I then resolved to sit down in the quiet of domestick life, and addressed[4] a lady that was fond of my conversation, but rejected my suit, because my father was a merchant.

'Wearied at last with solicitation and repulses, I resolved to hide myself for ever from the world, and depend no longer on the opinion or caprice of others. I waited for the time when the gate of the Happy Valley should open, that I might bid farewell to hope and fear: the day came; my performance was distinguished with favour, and I resigned myself with joy to perpetual confinement.'

'Hast thou here found happiness at last?' said Rasselas. 'Tell me without reserve; art thou content with thy condition? or, dost thou wish to be again wandering and enquiring? All the inhabitants of this valley celebrate their lot, and, at the annual visit of the emperour, invite others to partake of their felicity.'

'Great prince,' said Imlac, 'I shall speak the truth: I know not one of all your attendants who does not lament the hour when he entered this retreat. I am less unhappy than the rest, because I have a mind replete with images, which I can vary and combine at pleasure. I can amuse my solitude by the renovation of the knowledge which begins to fade from my memory, and by recollection of the accidents of my past life. Yet all this ends in the sorrowful consideration, that my acquirements are now useless, and that none of my pleasures can be again enjoyed. The rest, whose minds have no impression but of the present moment, are either corroded by malignant passions, or sit stupid in the gloom of perpetual vacancy.'

'What passions can infest those,' said the prince, 'who have no rivals? We are in a place where impotence precludes malice, and where all envy is repressed by community of enjoyments.'

'There may be community,' said Imlac, 'of material possessions, but there can never be community of love or of esteem. It must happen that one will please more than another; he that knows himself despised will always be envious; and still more envious and malevolent, if he is condemned to live in the presence of those who despise him. The invitations, by which they allure others to a state which they feel to be wretched, proceed from the natural malignity of hopeless misery. They are weary of themselves, and of each other, and expect to find relief in new companions. They envy the liberty which their folly has forfeited, and would gladly see all mankind imprisoned like themselves.

'From this crime, however, I am wholly free. No man can say that he is wretched by my persuasion. I look with pity on the crowds who are annually soliciting admission to captivity, and wish that it were lawful for me to warn them of their danger.'

'My dear Imlac,' said the prince, 'I will open to thee my whole heart. I have long meditated an escape from the Happy Valley. I have examined the mountains on every side, but find myself insuperably barred: teach me the way to break my prison; thou shalt be the companion of my flight, the guide of my rambles, the partner of my fortune, and my sole director in the *choice of life*.'

'Sir,' answered the poet, 'your escape will be difficult, and, perhaps, you may soon repent your curiosity. The world, which you figure to yourself smooth and quiet as the lake in the valley, you will find a sea foaming with tempests, and boiling with whirlpools: you will be sometimes overwhelmed by the waves of violence, and sometimes dashed against the rocks of treachery. Amidst wrongs and frauds, competitions and anxieties, you will wish a thousand times for these seats of quiet, and willingly quit hope to be free from fear.'

'Do not seek to deter me from my purpose,' said the prince: 'I am impatient to see what thou hast seen; and, since thou art thyself weary of the valley, it is evident, that thy former state was better than this. Whatever be the consequence of my experiment, I am resolved to judge with my own eyes of the various conditions of men, and then to make deliberately my *choice of life*.'

'I am afraid,' said Imlac, 'you are hindered by stronger restraints than my persuasions; yet, if your determination is fixed, I do not counsel you to despair. Few things are impossible to diligence and skill.'

CHAP. XIII

Rasselas discovers the means of escape

The prince now dismissed his favourite to rest, but the narrative of wonders and novelties filled his mind with perturbation.[1] He revolved all that he had heard, and prepared innumerable questions for the morning.

Much of his uneasiness was now removed. He had a friend to whom he could impart his thoughts, and whose experience could assist him in his designs. His heart was no longer condemned to swell with silent vexation. He thought that even the Happy Valley might be endured with such a companion, and that, if they could range the world together, he should have nothing further to desire.

In a few days the water was discharged, and the ground dried. The prince and Imlac then walked out together to converse without the notice of the rest. The prince, whose thoughts were always on the wing, as he passed by the gate, said, with a countenance of sorrow, 'Why art thou so strong, and why is man so weak?'

'Man is not weak,' answered his companion; 'knowledge is more than equivalent to force. The master of mechanicks laughs at strength. I can burst the gate, but cannot do it secretly. Some other expedient must be tried.'

As they were walking on the side of the mountain, they observed that the conies,[2] which the rain had driven from their burrows, had taken shelter among the bushes, and formed holes behind them, tending upwards in an oblique line. 'It has been the opinion of antiquity,' said Imlac, 'that human reason borrowed many arts from the instinct of animals;[3] let us, therefore, not think ourselves degraded by learning from the coney. We may escape by piercing the mountain in the same direction. We will begin where the summit hangs over the middle part, and labour upward till we shall issue out beyond the prominence.'

The eyes of the prince, when he heard this proposal, sparkled with joy. The execution was easy, and the success certain.

No time was now lost. They hastened early in the morning to chuse a place proper for their mine. They clambered with great fatigue among crags and brambles, and returned without having discovered any part that favoured their design. The second and the third day were spent in the same manner, and with the same frustration. But, on the fourth, they found a small cavern, concealed by a thicket, where they resolved to make their experiment.

Imlac procured instruments proper to hew stone and remove earth, and they fell to their work on the next day with more eagerness than vigour. They were presently exhausted by their efforts, and sat down to pant upon the grass. The prince, for a moment, appeared to be discouraged. 'Sir,' said his companion, 'practice will enable us to continue our labour for a longer time; mark, however, how far we have advanced, and you will find that our toil will some time have an end. Great works are performed, not by strength, but perseverance: yonder palace was raised by single stones, yet you see its height and spaciousness. He that shall walk with vigour three hours a day will pass in seven years a space equal to the circumference of the globe.'[4]

They returned to their work day after day, and, in a short time, found a fissure in the rock, which enabled them to pass far with very little obstruction. This Rasselas considered as a good omen. 'Do not disturb your mind,' said Imlac, 'with other hopes or fears than reason may suggest: if you are pleased with prognosticks of good, you will be terrified likewise with tokens of evil, and your whole life will be a prey to superstition.[5] Whatever facilitates our work is more than an omen, it is a cause of success. This is one of those pleasing surprises which often happen to active resolution. Many things difficult to design prove easy to performance.'

CHAP. XIV

Rasselas and Imlac receive an unexpected visit

They had now wrought their way to the middle, and solaced their toil with the approach of liberty, when the prince, coming down to refresh himself with air, found his sister Nekayah standing before the mouth of the cavity. He started and stood confused, afraid to tell his design, and yet hopeless to conceal it. A few moments determined him to repose[1] on her fidelity, and secure her secrecy by a declaration without reserve.

'Do not imagine,' said the princess, 'that I came hither as a spy: I had long observed from my window, that you and Imlac directed your walk every day towards the same point, but I did not suppose you had any better reason for the preference than a cooler shade, or more fragrant bank; nor followed you with any other design than to partake of your conversation. Since then not suspicion but fondness has detected you, let me not lose the advantage of my discovery. I am equally weary of confinement with yourself, and not less desirous of knowing what is done or suffered in the world. Permit me to fly with you from this tasteless tranquility, which will yet grow more loathsome when you have left me. You may deny me to accompany you, but cannot hinder me from following.'

The prince, who loved Nekayah above his other sisters, had no inclination to refuse her request, and grieved that he had lost an opportunity of shewing his confidence by a voluntary communication. It was therefore agreed that she should leave the valley with them; and that, in the mean time, she should watch, lest any other straggler[2] should, by chance or curiosity, follow them to the mountain.

At length their labour was at an end; they saw light beyond the prominence, and, issuing to the top of the mountain, beheld the Nile, yet a narrow current, wandering beneath them.

The prince looked round with rapture, anticipated all the pleasures of travel, and in thought was already transported beyond his father's dominions. Imlac, though very joyful at his escape, had less expectation of pleasure in the world, which he had before tried, and of which he had been weary.

Rasselas was so much delighted with a wider horizon, that he could not soon be persuaded to return into the valley. He informed his sister that the way was open, and that nothing now remained but to prepare for their departure.

CHAP. XV

The prince and princess leave the valley, and see many wonders

The prince and princess had jewels sufficient to make them rich whenever they came into a place of commerce, which, by Imlac's direction, they hid in their cloaths, and, on the night of the next full moon, all left the valley. The princess was followed only by a single favourite, who did not know whither she was going.

They clambered through the cavity, and began to go down on the other side. The princess and her maid turned their eyes towards every part, and, seeing nothing to bound their prospect, considered themselves as in danger of being lost in a dreary vacuity. They stopped and trembled. 'I am almost afraid,' said the princess, 'to begin a journey of which I cannot perceive an end, and to venture into this immense plain where I may be approached on every side by men whom I never saw.' The prince felt nearly the same emotions, though he thought it more manly to conceal them.

Imlac smiled at their terrours, and encouraged them to proceed; but the princess continued irresolute till she had been imperceptibly drawn forward too far to return.

In the morning they found some shepherds in the field, who set milk and fruits before them. The princess wondered that she did not see a palace ready for her reception, and a table spread with delicacies; but, being faint and hungry, she drank the milk and eat[1] the fruits, and thought them of a higher flavour than the products of the valley.

They travelled forward by easy journeys, being all unaccustomed to toil or difficulty, and knowing, that though they might be missed, they could not be persued. In a few days they came into a more populous region, where Imlac was diverted with the admiration which his companions expressed at the diversity of manners, stations and employments.

Their dress was such as might not bring upon them the suspicion of having any thing to conceal, yet the prince, wherever he came, expected to be obeyed, and the princess was frighted, because those that came into her presence did not prostrate themselves before her. Imlac was forced to observe them with great vigilance, lest they should betray their rank by their unusual behaviour, and detained them several weeks in the first village to accustom them to the sight of common mortals.

By degrees the royal wanderers were taught to understand

that they had for a time laid aside their dignity,[2] and were to expect only such regard as liberality and courtesy could procure. And Imlac, having, by many admonitions, prepared them to endure the tumults of a port, and the ruggedness of the commercial race,[3] brought them down to the sea-coast.

The prince and his sister, to whom every thing was new, were gratified equally at all places, and therefore remained for some months at the port without any inclination to pass further. Imlac was content with their stay, because he did not think it safe to expose them, unpractised in the world, to the hazards of a foreign country.

At last he began to fear lest they should be discovered, and proposed to fix a day for their departure. They had no pretensions to judge for themselves, and referred the whole scheme to his direction. He therefore took passage in a ship to Suez; and, when the time came, with great difficulty prevailed on the princess to enter the vessel. They had a quick and prosperous voyage, and from Suez travelled by land to Cairo.

CHAP. XVI

They enter Cairo, and find every man happy

As they approached the city, which filled the strangers with astonishment, 'This,' said Imlac to the prince, 'is the place where travellers and merchants assemble from all the corners of the earth. You will here find men of every character, and every occupation. Commerce is here honourable:[1] I will act as a merchant, and you shall live as strangers, who have no other end of travel than curiosity; it will soon be observed that we are rich; our reputation will procure us access to all whom we shall desire to know; you will see all the conditions of humanity, and enable yourself at leisure to make your *choice of life*.'

They now entered the town, stunned by the noise, and offended[2] by the crowds. Instruction had not yet so prevailed over habit, but that they wondered to see themselves pass undistinguished along the street, and met by the lowest of the people without reverence or notice. The princess could not at first bear the thought of being levelled with the vulgar, and, for some days, continued in her chamber, where she was served by her favourite Pekuah as in the palace of the valley.

Imlac, who understood traffick,[3] sold part of the jewels the next day, and hired a house, which he adorned with such magnificence, that he was immediately considered as a merchant of great wealth. His politeness attracted many acquaintance,[4] and his generosity made him courted by many dependants. His table was crowded by men of every nation, who all admired his knowledge, and solicited his favour. His companions, not being able to mix in the conversation, could make no discovery[5] of their ignorance or surprise, and were gradually initiated in the world as they gained knowledge of the language.

The prince had, by frequent lectures, been taught the use and nature of money; but the ladies could not, for a long time, comprehend what the merchants did with small pieces of gold and silver, or why things of so little use should be received as equivalent to the necessaries of life.

They studied the language two years, while Imlac was preparing to set before them the various ranks and conditions of mankind. He grew acquainted with all who had any thing uncommon in their fortune or conduct. He frequented the voluptuous[6] and the frugal, the idle and the busy, the merchants and the men of learning.

The prince, being now able to converse with fluency, and having learned the caution necessary to be observed in his intercourse with strangers, began to accompany Imlac to places of resort, and to enter into all assemblies, that he might make his *choice of life*.

For some time he thought choice needless, because all appeared to him equally happy. Wherever he went he met gaiety and kindness, and heard the song of joy, or the laugh of carelessness. He began to believe that the world overflowed with universal plenty, and that nothing was withheld either from want or merit; that every hand showered liberality, and every heart melted with benevolence: 'and who then,' says he, 'will be suffered to be wretched?'

Imlac permitted the pleasing delusion, and was unwilling to crush the hope of inexperience, till one day, having sat a while silent, 'I know not,' said the prince, 'what can be the reason that I am more unhappy than any of our friends. I see them perpetually and unalterably chearful, but feel my own mind restless and uneasy. I am unsatisfied with those pleasures which I seem most to court; I live in the crowds of jollity, not so much to enjoy company as to shun myself, and am only loud and merry to conceal my sadness.'

'Every man,' said Imlac, 'may, by examining his own mind, guess what passes in the minds of others: when you feel that your own gaiety is counterfeit, it may justly lead you to suspect that of your companions not to be sincere. Envy is commonly reciprocal. We are long before we are convinced that happiness is never to be found, and each believes it possessed by others, to keep alive the hope of obtaining it for himself. In the assembly, where you passed the last night, there appeared such spriteliness of air, and volatility of fancy, as might have suited beings of an higher order, formed to inhabit serener regions inaccessible to care or sorrow: yet, believe me, prince, there was not one who did not dread the moment when solitude should deliver him to the tyranny of reflection.'[7]

'This,' said the prince, 'may be true of others, since it is true of me; yet, whatever be the general infelicity of man, one condition is more happy than another, and wisdom surely directs us to take the least evil in the *choice of life*.'

'The causes of good and evil,' answered Imlac, 'are so various and uncertain, so often entangled with each other, so diversified by various relations, and so much subject to accidents which cannot be foreseen, that he who would fix his condition upon incontestable reasons of preference, must live and die enquiring and deliberating.'

'But surely,' said Rasselas, 'the wise men, to whom we listen with reverence and wonder, chose that mode of life for themselves which they thought most likely to make them happy.'

'Very few,' said the poet, 'live by choice. Every man is placed

determination

in his present condition by causes which acted without his foresight, and with which he did not always willingly co-operate; and therefore you will rarely meet one who does not think the lot of his neighbour better than his own.'

'I am pleased to think,' said the prince, 'that my birth has given me at least one advantage over others, by enabling me to determine for myself. I have here the world before me; I will review it at leisure: surely happiness is somewhere to be found.'

CHAP. XVII

The prince associates with young men of spirit and gaiety

Rasselas rose next day, and resolved to begin his experiments upon life. 'Youth,' cried he, 'is the time of gladness: I will join myself to the young men, whose only business is to gratify their desires, and whose time is all spent in a succession of enjoyments.'

To such societies he was readily admitted, but a few days brought him back weary and disgusted. Their mirth was without images,[1] their laughter without motive; their pleasures were gross and sensual, in which the mind had no part; their conduct was at once wild and mean; they laughed at order and at law, but the frown of power dejected, and the eye of wisdom abashed them.

The prince soon concluded, that he should never be happy in a course of life of which he was ashamed. He thought it unsuitable to a reasonable being to act without a plan, and to be sad or chearful only by chance. 'Happiness,' said he, 'must be something solid and permanent, without fear and without uncertainty.'[2]

But his young companions had gained so much of his regard by their frankness and courtesy, that he could not leave them without warning and remonstrance. 'My friends,' said he, 'I have seriously considered our manners and our prospects, and find that we have mistaken our own interest. The first years of man must make provision for the last. He that never thinks never can be wise. Perpetual levity must end in ignorance; and intemperance, though it may fire the spirits for an hour, will make life short or miserable. Let us consider that youth is of no long duration, and that in maturer age, when the enchantments of fancy shall cease, and phantoms of delight dance no more about us, we shall have no comforts but the esteem of wise men, and the means of doing good. Let us, therefore, stop, while to stop is in our power: let us live as men who are sometime to grow old, and to whom it will be the most dreadful of all evils not to count their past years but by follies, and to be reminded of their former luxuriance of health only by the maladies which riot[3] has produced.'

They stared a while in silence one upon another, and, at last, drove him away by a general chorus of continued laughter.

The consciousness that his sentiments were just, and his intentions kind, was scarcely sufficient to support him against the horrour of derision. But he recovered his tranquility, and persued his search.

CHAP. XVIII

The prince finds a wise and happy man

As he was one day walking in the street, he saw a spacious building which all were, by the open doors, invited to enter: he followed the stream of people, and found it a hall or school of declamation, in which professors read lectures to their auditory.[1] He fixed his eye upon a sage raised above the rest, who discoursed with great energy on the government of the passions.[2] His look was venerable, his action graceful, his pronunciation clear, and his diction elegant. He shewed, with great strength of sentiment, and variety of illustration, that human nature is degraded and debased, when the lower faculties predominate over the higher; that when fancy, the parent of passion, usurps the dominion of the mind, nothing ensues but the natural effect of unlawful government, perturbation and confusion; that she betrays the fortresses of the intellect to rebels, and excites her children to sedition against reason their lawful sovereign. He compared reason to the sun, of which the light is constant, uniform, and lasting; and fancy to a meteor, of bright but transitory lustre, irregular in its motion, and delusive in its direction.

He then communicated the various precepts given from time to time for the conquest of passion, and displayed the happiness of those who had obtained the important victory, after which man is no longer the slave of fear, nor the fool of hope; is no more emaciated by envy, inflamed by anger, emasculated by tenderness, or depressed by grief; but walks on calmly through the tumults or the privacies of life, as the sun persues alike his course through the calm or the stormy sky.

He enumerated many examples of heroes immovable by pain or pleasure, who looked with indifference on those modes or accidents to which the vulgar give the names of good and evil. He exhorted his hearers to lay aside their prejudices, and arm themselves against the shafts of malice or misfortune, by invulnerable patience; concluding, that this state only was happiness, and that this happiness was in every one's power.

Rasselas listened to him with the veneration due to the instructions of a superiour being, and, waiting for him at the door, humbly implored the liberty of visiting so great a master of true wisdom. The lecturer hesitated a moment, when Rasselas put a purse of gold into his hand, which he received with a mixture of joy and wonder.

'I have found,' said the prince, at his return to Imlac, 'a man who can teach all that is necessary to be known, who, from the unshaken throne of rational fortitude, looks down on the scenes of life changing beneath him. He speaks, and attention watches his lips. He reasons, and conviction closes his periods. This man shall be my future guide: I will learn his doctrines, and imitate his life.'

'Be not too hasty,' said Imlac, 'to trust, or to admire, the teachers of morality: they discourse like angels, but they live like men.'

Rasselas, who could not conceive how any man could reason so forcibly without feeling the cogency of his own arguments, paid his visit in a few days, and was denied admission. He had now learned the power of money, and made his way by a piece of gold to the inner apartment, where he found the philosopher in a room half darkened, with his eyes misty, and his face pale. 'Sir,' said he, 'you are come at a time when all human friendship is useless; what I suffer cannot be remedied, what I have lost cannot be supplied. My daughter, my only daughter, from whose tenderness I expected all the comforts of my age, died last night of a fever. My views, my purposes, my hopes are at an end: I am now a lonely being disunited from society.'

'Sir,' said the prince, 'mortality is an event by which a wise man can never be surprised: we know that death is always near, and it should therefore always be expected.' 'Young man,' answered the philosopher, 'you speak like one that has never felt the pangs of separation.' 'Have you then forgot the precepts,' said Rasselas, 'which you so powerfully enforced? Has wisdom no strength to arm the heart against calamity? Consider, that external things are naturally variable, but truth and reason are always the same.' 'What comfort,' said the mourner, 'can truth and reason afford me? of what effect are they now, but to tell me, that my daughter will not be restored?'

The prince, whose humanity would not suffer him to insult misery with reproof, went away convinced of the emptiness of rhetorical sound, and the inefficacy of polished periods and studied sentences.

CHAP. XIX

A glimpse of pastoral life

He was still eager upon the same enquiry; and, having heard of
a hermit, that lived near the lowest cataract of the Nile,[1] and
filled the whole country with the fame of his sanctity, resolved
to visit his retreat, and enquire whether that felicity, which
publick life could not afford, was to be found in solitude; and
whether a man, whose age and virtue made him venerable,
could teach any peculiar art of shunning evils, or enduring
them.

Imlac and the princess agreed to accompany him, and, after
the necessary preparations, they began their journey. Their way
lay through fields, where shepherds tended their flocks, and the
lambs were playing upon the pasture. 'This,' said the poet, 'is
the life which has been often celebrated for its innocence and
quiet: let us pass the heat of the day among the shepherds' tents,
and know whether all our searches are not to terminate in
pastoral simplicity.'

The proposal pleased them, and they induced the shepherds,
by small presents and familiar questions, to tell their opinion
of their own state: they were so rude and ignorant, so little able
to compare the good with the evil of the occupation, and so
indistinct in their narratives and descriptions, that very little
could be learned from them. But it was evident that their hearts
were cankered with discontent; that they considered themselves
as condemned to labour for the luxury of the rich, and looked
up with stupid malevolence toward those that were placed
above them.

The princess pronounced with vehemence, that she would
never suffer these envious savages to be her companions, and
that she should not soon be desirous of seeing any more speci-
mens of rustick happiness; but could not believe that all the
accounts of primeval pleasures were fabulous, and was yet in
doubt whether life had any thing that could be justly preferred
to the placid gratifications of fields and woods. She hoped that

the time would come, when, with a few virtuous and elegant companions, she should gather flowers planted by her own hand, fondle the lambs of her own ewe, and listen, without care, among brooks and breezes, to one of her maidens reading in the shade.[2]

CHAP. XX

The danger of prosperity

On the next day they continued their journey, till the heat compelled them to look round for shelter. At a small distance they saw a thick wood, which they no sooner entered than they perceived that they were approaching the habitations of men.[1] The shrubs were diligently cut away to open walks where the shades were darkest; the boughs of opposite trees were artificially interwoven; seats of flowery turf were raised in vacant spaces, and a rivulet, that wantoned[2] along the side of a winding path, had its banks sometimes opened into small basons, and its stream sometimes obstructed by little mounds of stone heaped together to increase its murmurs.

They passed slowly through the wood, delighted with such unexpected accommodations, and entertained each other with conjecturing what, or who, he could be, that, in those rude and unfrequented regions, had leisure and art for such harmless luxury.

As they advanced, they heard the sound of musick, and saw youths and virgins[3] dancing in the grove; and, going still further, beheld a stately palace built upon a hill surrounded with woods. The laws of eastern hospitality allowed them to enter,[4] and the master welcomed them like a man liberal and wealthy.

He was skilful enough in appearances soon to discern that they were no common guests, and spread his table with magnificence. The eloquence of Imlac caught his attention, and the lofty courtesy of the princess excited his respect. When they offered to depart he entreated their stay, and was the next day still more unwilling to dismiss them than before. They were easily persuaded to stop, and civility grew up in time to freedom and confidence.

The prince now saw all the domesticks chearful, and all the face of nature smiling round the place, and could not forbear to hope that he should find here what he was seeking; but when he was congratulating the master upon his possessions, he answered with a sigh, 'My condition has indeed the appearance of happiness, but appearances are delusive. My prosperity puts my life in danger; the Bassa of Egypt[5] is my enemy, incensed only by my wealth and popularity. I have been hitherto protected against him by the princes of the country; but, as the favour of the great is uncertain, I know not how soon my defenders may be persuaded to share the plunder with the Bassa.[6] I have sent my treasures into a distant country, and, upon the first alarm, am prepared to follow them. Then will my enemies riot[7] in my mansion, and enjoy the gardens which I have planted.'

They all joined in lamenting his danger, and deprecating his exile; and the princess was so much disturbed with the tumult of grief and indignation, that she retired to her apartment. They continued with their kind inviter a few days longer, and then went forward to find the hermit.

CHAP. XXI

The happiness of solitude.[1] *The hermit's history*

They came on the third day, by the direction of the peasants, to the hermit's cell: it was a cavern in the side of a mountain, over-shadowed with palm-trees; at such a distance from the cataract, that nothing more was heard than a gentle uniform murmur, such as composed the mind to pensive meditation, especially when it was assisted by the wind whistling among the branches. The first rude essay of nature had been so much improved by human labour, that the cave contained several

apartments, appropriated to different uses, and often afforded lodging to travellers, whom darkness or tempests happened to overtake.

The hermit sat on a bench at the door, to enjoy the coolness of the evening. On one side lay a book with pens and papers, on the other mechanical instruments of various kinds. As they approached him unregarded, the princess observed that he had not the countenance of a man that had found, or could teach, the way to happiness.

They saluted[2] him with great respect, which he repaid like a man not unaccustomed to the forms of courts. 'My children,' said he, 'if you have lost your way, you shall be willingly supplied with such conveniencies for the night as this cavern will afford. I have all that nature requires, and you will not expect delicacies in a hermit's cell.'

They thanked him, and, entering, were pleased with the neatness and regularity of the place. The hermit set flesh and wine before them, though he fed only upon fruits and water. His discourse was chearful without levity, and pious without enthusiasm.[3] He soon gained the esteem of his guests, and the princess repented of her hasty censure.

At last Imlac began thus: 'I do not now wonder that your reputation is so far extended; we have heard at Cairo of your wisdom, and came hither to implore your direction for this young man and maiden in the *choice of life.*'

'To him that lives well,' answered the hermit, 'every form of life is good; nor can I give any other rule for choice, than to remove from all apparent evil.'

'He will remove most certainly from evil,' said the prince, 'who shall devote himself to that solitude which you have recommended by your example.'

'I have indeed lived fifteen years in solitude,' said the hermit, 'but have no desire that my example should gain any imitators. In my youth I professed arms,[4] and was raised by degrees to the highest military rank. I have traversed wide countries at the head of my troops, and seen many battles and sieges. At last, being disgusted by the preferments of a younger officer, and feeling that my vigour was beginning to decay, I resolved to

close my life in peace, having found the world full of snares, discord, and misery. I had once escaped from the persuit of the enemy by the shelter of this cavern, and therefore chose it for my final residence. I employed artificers to form it into chambers, and stored it with all that I was likely to want.

'For some time after my retreat, I rejoiced like a tempest-beaten sailor at his entrance into the harbour, being delighted with the sudden change of the noise and hurry of war, to stillness and repose. When the pleasure of novelty went away, I employed my hours in examining the plants which grow in the valley, and the minerals which I collected from the rocks. But that enquiry is now grown tasteless and irksome. I have been for some time unsettled and distracted: my mind is disturbed with a thousand perplexities of doubt, and vanities of imagination, which hourly prevail upon me, because I have no opportunities of relaxation or diversion. I am sometimes ashamed to think that I could not secure myself from vice, but by retiring from the exercise of virtue, and begin to suspect that I was rather impelled by resentment, than led by devotion, into solitude. My fancy riots in scenes of folly,[5] and I lament that I have lost so much, and have gained so little. In solitude, if I escape the example of bad men, I want likewise the counsel and conversation of the good. I have been long comparing the evils with the advantages of society, and resolve to return into the world to morrow. The life of a solitary man will be certainly miserable, but not certainly devout.'

They heard his resolution with surprise, but, after a short pause, offered to conduct him to Cairo. He dug up a considerable treasure which he had hid among the rocks, and accompanied them to the city, on which, as he approached it, he gazed with rapture.

CHAP. XXII

The happiness of a life led according to nature[1]

Rasselas went often to an assembly of learned men, who met at stated times to unbend their minds, and compare their opinions. Their manners were somewhat coarse, but their conversation was instructive, and their disputations acute, though sometimes too violent, and often continued till neither controvertist[2] remembered upon what question they began. Some faults were almost general among them: every one was desirous to dictate to the rest, and every one was pleased to hear the genius or knowledge of another depreciated.

In this assembly Rasselas was relating his interview with the hermit, and the wonder with which he heard him censure a course of life which he had so deliberately chosen, and so laudably followed. The sentiments of the hearers were various. Some were of opinion, that the folly of his choice had been justly punished by condemnation to perpetual perseverance. One of the youngest among them, with great vehemence, pronounced him an hypocrite. Some talked of the right of society to the labour of individuals, and considered retirement as a desertion of duty.[3] Others readily allowed, that there was a time when the claims of the publick were satisfied, and when a man might properly sequester himself, to review his life, and purify his heart.[4]

One, who appeared more affected with the narrative than the rest, thought it likely, that the hermit would, in a few years, go back to his retreat, and, perhaps, if shame did not restrain, or death intercept him, return once more from his retreat into the world: 'For the hope of happiness,' said he, 'is so strongly impressed, that the longest experience is not able to efface it. Of the present state, whatever it be, we feel, and are forced to confess, the misery, yet, when the same state is again at a distance, imagination paints it as desirable. But the time will surely come, when desire will be no longer our torment, and no man shall be wretched but by his own fault.'[5]

'This,' said a philosopher, who had heard him with tokens of great impatience, 'is the present condition of a wise man. The time is already come, when none are wretched but by their own fault. Nothing is more idle, than to enquire after happiness, which nature has kindly placed within our reach. The way to be happy is to live according to nature, in obedience to that universal and unalterable law with which every heart is originally impressed; which is not written on it by precept, but engraven by destiny, not instilled by education, but infused at our nativity.[6] He that lives according to nature will suffer nothing from the delusions of hope, or importunities of desire: he will receive and reject with equability of temper; and act or suffer as the reason of things shall alternately prescribe. Other men may amuse themselves with subtle definitions, or intricate raciocination. Let them learn to be wise by easier means: let them observe the hind of the forest, and the linnet of the grove: let them consider the life of animals, whose motions are regulated by instinct; they obey their guide and are happy.[7] Let us therefore, at length, cease to dispute, and learn to live; throw away the incumbrance of precepts, which they who utter them with so much pride and pomp do not understand, and carry with us this simple and intelligible maxim, that deviation from nature is deviation from happiness.'

When he had spoken, he looked round him with a placid air, and enjoyed the consciousness of his own beneficence. 'Sir,' said the prince, with great modesty, 'as I, like all the rest of mankind, am desirous of felicity, my closest attention has been fixed upon your discourse: I doubt not the truth of a position which a man so learned has so confidently advanced. Let me only know what it is to live according to nature.'

'When I find young men so humble and so docile,' said the philosopher, 'I can deny them no information which my studies have enabled me to afford. To live according to nature, is to act always with due regard to the fitness[8] arising from the relations and qualities of causes and effects; to concur with the great and unchangeable scheme of universal felicity; to co-operate with the general disposition and tendency of the present system of things.'

The prince soon found that this was one of the sages whom he should understand less as he heard him longer. He therefore bowed and was silent, and the philosopher, supposing him satisfied, and the rest vanquished, rose up and departed with the air of a man that had co-operated with the present system.

CHAP. XXIII

The prince and his sister divide between them the work of observation

Rasselas returned home full of reflexions, doubtful how to direct his future steps. Of the way to happiness he found the learned and simple equally ignorant; but, as he was yet young,[1] he flattered himself that he had time remaining for more experiments, and further enquiries. He communicated to Imlac his observations and his doubts, but was answered by him with new doubts, and remarks that gave him no comfort. He therefore discoursed more frequently and freely with his sister, who had yet the same hope with himself, and always assisted him to give some reason why, though he had been hitherto frustrated, he might succeed at last.

'We have hitherto,' said she, 'known but little of the world: we have never yet been either great or mean. In our own country, though we had royalty, we had no power, and in this we have not yet seen the private recesses of domestick peace. Imlac favours not our search, lest we should in time find him mistaken. We will divide the task between us: you shall try what is to be found in the splendour of courts, and I will range the shades of humbler life. Perhaps command and authority may be the supreme blessings, as they afford most opportunities of doing good: or, perhaps, what this world can give may be found in the modest habitations of middle fortune; too low for great designs, and too high for penury and distress.'

CHAP. XXIV

The prince examines the happiness of high stations

Rasselas applauded the design, and appeared next day with a splendid retinue at the court of the Bassa. He was soon distinguished for his magnificence, and admitted, as a prince whose curiosity had brought him from distant countries, to an intimacy with the great officers, and frequent conversation with the Bassa himself.

He was at first inclined to believe, that the man must be pleased with his own condition, whom all approached with reverence, and heard with obedience, and who had the power to extend his edicts to a whole kingdom. 'There can be no pleasure,' said he, 'equal to that of feeling at once the joy of thousands all made happy by wise administration. Yet, since, by the law of subordination, this sublime delight can be in one nation but the lot of one, it is surely reasonable to think that there is some satisfaction more popular[1] and accessible, and that millions can hardly be subjected to the will of a single man, only to fill his particular breast with incommunicable content.'

These thoughts were often in his mind, and he found no solution of the difficulty. But as presents and civilities gained him more familiarity, he found that almost every man who stood high in employment hated all the rest, and was hated by them, and that their lives were a continual succession of plots and detections, stratagems and escapes, faction and treachery. Many of those, who surrounded the Bassa, were sent only to watch and report his conduct; every tongue was muttering censure, and every eye was searching for a fault.

At last the letters of revocation[2] arrived, the Bassa was carried in chains to Constantinople,[3] and his name was mentioned no more.

'What are we now to think of the prerogatives of power,' said Rasselas to his sister; 'is it without any efficacy to good? or, is the subordinate degree only dangerous, and the supreme safe and glorious? Is the Sultan[4] the only happy man in his dominions? or, is the Sultan himself subject to the torments of suspicion, and the dread of enemies?'

In a short time the second Bassa was deposed. The Sultan, that had advanced him, was murdered by the Janisaries,[5] and his successor had other views and different favourites.

CHAP. XXV

The princess persues her enquiry with more diligence than success

The princess, in the mean time, insinuated herself[1] into many families; for there are few doors, through which liberality, joined with good humour, cannot find its way. The daughters of many houses were airy[2] and chearful, but Nekayah had been too long accustomed to the conversation of Imlac and her brother to be much pleased with childish levity and prattle which had no meaning. She found their thoughts narrow, their wishes low, and their merriment often artificial. Their pleasures, poor as they were, could not be preserved pure, but were embittered by petty competitions and worthless emulation. They were always jealous of the beauty of each other; of a quality to which solicitude can add nothing, and from which detraction can take nothing away. Many were in love with triflers like themselves, and many fancied that they were in love when in truth they were only idle. Their affection was seldom fixed on sense or virtue, and therefore seldom ended but in vexation. Their grief, however, like their joy, was transient; every thing floated in their mind unconnected with the past or future, so that one desire easily gave way to another, as a second stone cast into the water effaces and confounds the circles of the first.

With these girls she played as with inoffensive animals, and found them proud of her countenance,[3] and weary of her company.

But her purpose was to examine more deeply, and her affability easily persuaded the hearts that were swelling with sorrow to discharge their secrets in her ear: and those whom hope flattered, or prosperity delighted, often courted her to partake their pleasures.

The princess and her brother commonly met in the evening in a private summerhouse on the bank of the Nile, and related to each other the occurrences of the day. As they were sitting together, the princess cast her eyes upon the river that flowed before her. 'Answer,' said she, 'great father of waters,[4] thou that rollest thy floods through eighty nations, to the invocations of the daughter of thy native king. Tell me if thou waterest, through all thy course, a single habitation from which thou dost not hear the murmurs of complaint?'

'You are then,' said Rasselas, 'not more successful in private houses than I have been in courts.' 'I have, since the last partition of our provinces,[5] said the princess, 'enabled myself to enter familiarly into many families, where there was the fairest show of prosperity and peace, and know not one house that is not haunted by some fury that destroys its quiet.

'I did not seek ease among the poor, because I concluded that there it could not be found.[6] But I saw many poor whom I had supposed to live in affluence. Poverty has, in large cities, very different appearances: it is often concealed in splendour, and often in extravagance. It is the care of a very great part of mankind to conceal their indigence from the rest: they support themselves by temporary expedients, and every day is lost in contriving for the morrow.[7]

'This, however, was an evil, which, though frequent, I saw with less pain, because I could relieve it. Yet some have refused my bounties; more offended with my quickness to detect their wants, than pleased with my readiness to succour them: and others, whose exigencies compelled them to admit my kindness, have never been able to forgive their benefactress. Many, however, have been sincerely grateful without the ostentation of gratitude, or the hope of other favours.'

END OF THE FIRST VOLUME.

CHAP. XXVI

The princess continues her remarks upon private life

Nekayah perceiving her brother's attention fixed, proceeded in her narrative.

'In families, where there is or is not poverty, there is commonly discord: if a kingdom be, as Imlac tells us, a great family, a family likewise is a little kingdom, torn with factions and exposed to revolutions. An unpractised observer expects the love of parents and children to be constant and equal; but this kindness seldom continues beyond the years of infancy: in a short time the children become rivals to their parents. Benefits are allayed[1] by reproaches, and gratitude debased by envy.

'Parents and children seldom act in concert: each child endeavours to appropriate the esteem or fondness of the parents, and the parents, with yet less temptation, betray each other to their children; thus some place their confidence in the father, and some in the mother, and, by degrees, the house is filled with artifices and feuds.

'The opinions of children and parents, of the young and the old, are naturally opposite, by the contrary effects of hope and despondence, of expectation and experience, without crime or folly on either side. The colours of life in youth and age appear different, as the face of nature in spring and winter. And how can children credit the assertions of parents, which their own eyes show them to be false?

'Few parents act in such a manner as much to enforce their maxims by the credit of their lives. The old man trusts wholly to slow contrivance and gradual progression: the youth expects to force his way by genius, vigour, and precipitance. The old man pays regard to riches, and the youth reverences virtue. The old man deifies prudence: the youth commits himself to magnanimity and chance. The young man, who intends no ill, believes that none is intended, and therefore acts with openness and candour:[2] but his father, having suffered the injuries of fraud, is impelled to suspect, and too often allured to practise it. Age looks with anger on the temerity of youth, and youth with contempt on the scrupulosity of age. Thus parents and children, for the greatest part, live on to love less and less: and, if those whom nature has thus closely united are the torments of each other, where shall we look for tenderness and consolation?'

'Surely,' said the prince, 'you must have been unfortunate in your choice of acquaintance: I am unwilling to believe, that the most tender of all relations is thus impeded in its effects by natural necessity.'

'Domestick discord,' answered she, 'is not inevitably and fatally[3] necessary; but yet is not easily avoided. We seldom see that a whole family is virtuous: the good and evil cannot well agree; and the evil can yet less agree with one another: even the virtuous fall sometimes to variance, when their virtues are of different kinds, and tending to extremes. In general, those parents have most reverence who most deserve it: for he that lives well cannot be despised.

'Many other evils infest private life. Some are the slaves of servants whom they have trusted with their affairs. Some are kept in continual anxiety to the caprice of rich relations, whom they cannot please, and dare not offend. Some husbands are imperious, and some wives perverse: and, as it is always more easy to do evil than good, though the wisdom or virtue of one can very rarely make many happy, the folly or vice of one may often make many miserable.'

'If such be the general effect of marriage,' said the prince, 'I shall, for the future, think it dangerous to connect my interest with that of another, lest I should be unhappy by my partner's fault.'

'I have met,' said the princess, 'with many who live single for that reason; but I never found that their prudence ought to raise envy. They dream away their time without friendship, without fondness, and are driven to rid themselves of the day, for which they have no use, by childish amusements, or vicious delights. They act as beings under the constant sense of some known inferiority, that fills their minds with rancour, and their tongues with censure. They are peevish at home, and malevolent abroad; and, as the out-laws of human nature, make it their business and their pleasure to disturb that society which debars them from its privileges. To live without feeling or exciting sympathy, to be fortunate without adding to the felicity of others, or afflicted without tasting the balm of pity, is a state more gloomy than solitude: it is not retreat but exclusion from mankind. Marriage has many pains, but celibacy has no pleasures.'[4]

'What then is to be done?' said Rasselas; 'the more we enquire, the less we can resolve. Surely he is most likely to please himself that has no other inclination to regard.'

CHAP. XXVII

Disquisition upon greatness

The conversation had a short pause. The prince, having considered his sister's observations, told her, that she had surveyed life with prejudice, and supposed misery where she did not find it. 'Your narrative,' says he, 'throws yet a darker gloom upon the prospects of futurity: the predictions of Imlac were but faint sketches of the evils painted by Nekayah. I have been lately convinced that quiet is not the daughter of grandeur, or of power: that her presence is not to be bought by wealth, nor enforced by conquest. It is evident, that as any man acts in a wider compass, he must be more exposed to opposition from enmity or miscarriage from chance; whoever has many to please or to govern, must use the ministry of many agents, some of whom will be wicked, and some ignorant; by some he will be misled, and by others betrayed. If he gratifies one he will offend another: those that are not favoured will think themselves injured; and, since favours can be conferred but upon few, the greater number will be always discontented.'

'The discontent,' said the princess, 'which is thus unreasonable, I hope that I shall always have spirit to despise, and you, power to repress.'

'Discontent,' answered Rasselas, 'will not always be without reason under the most just or vigilant administration of publick affairs. None, however attentive, can always discover that merit which indigence or faction may happen to obscure; and none, however powerful, can always reward it. Yet, he that sees inferiour desert[1] advanced above him, will naturally impute that preference to partiality or caprice; and, indeed, it can scarcely be hoped that any man, however magnanimous by nature, or exalted by condition, will be able to persist for ever in fixed and inexorable justice of distribution: he will sometimes indulge his own affections, and sometimes those of his favourites; he will permit some to please him who can never serve him; he will discover in those whom he loves qualities which in reality they do not possess; and to those, from whom he receives pleasure, he will in his turn endeavour to give it. Thus will recommendations sometimes prevail which were purchased by money, or by the more destructive bribery of flattery and servility.

'He that has much to do will do something wrong, and of that wrong must suffer the consequences; and, if it were possible that he should always act rightly, yet when such numbers are to judge of his conduct, the bad will censure and obstruct him by malevolence, and the good sometimes by mistake.

'The highest stations cannot therefore hope to be the abodes of happiness, which I would willingly believe to have fled from thrones and palaces to seats of humble privacy and placid obscurity. For what can hinder the satisfaction, or intercept the expectations, of him whose abilities are adequate to his employments, who sees with his own eyes the whole circuit of his influence, who chooses by his own knowledge all whom he trusts, and whom none are tempted to deceive by hope or fear? Surely he has nothing to do but to love and to be loved, to be virtuous and to be happy.'

'Whether perfect happiness would be procured by perfect goodness,' said Nekayah, 'this world will never afford an opportunity of deciding. But this, at least, may be maintained, that we do not always find visible happiness in proportion to visible virtue. All natural and almost all political evils, are incident alike to the bad and good:[2] they are confounded in the misery of a famine, and not much distinguished in the fury of a faction; they sink together in a tempest, and are driven together from their country by invaders. All that virtue can afford is quietness of conscience, a steady prospect of a happier state; this may enable us to endure calamity with patience; but remember that patience must suppose pain.'

CHAP. XXVIII

Rasselas and Nekayah continue their conversation

'Dear princess,' said Rasselas, 'you fall into the common errours of exaggeratory declamation, by producing, in a familiar[1] disquisition, examples of national calamities, and scenes of extensive misery, which are found in books rather than in the world, and which, as they are horrid, are ordained to be rare. Let us not imagine evils which we do not feel, nor injure life by misrepresentations. I cannot bear that querulous eloquence which threatens every city with a siege like that of Jerusalem,[2] that makes famine attend on every flight of locusts, and suspends pestilence on the wing of every blast that issues from the south.

'On necessary and inevitable evils, which overwhelm kingdoms at once, all disputation is vain: when they happen they must be endured. But it is evident, that these bursts of universal distress are more dreaded than felt: thousands and ten thousands flourish in youth, and wither in age, without the knowledge of any other than domestick evils, and share the same pleasures and vexations whether their kings are mild or cruel, whether the armies of their country persue their enemies, or retreat before them. While courts are disturbed with intestine competitions, and ambassadours are negotiating in foreign countries, the smith still plies his anvil, and the husbandman drives his plow forward; the necessaries of life are required and obtained, and the successive business of the seasons continues to make its wonted revolutions.[3]

'Let us cease to consider what, perhaps, may never happen, and what, when it shall happen, will laugh at human specu-lation. We will not endeavour to modify the motions of the elements, or to fix the destiny of kingdoms. It is our business to consider what beings like us may perform; each labouring for his own happiness, by promoting within his circle, however narrow, the happiness of others.

'Marriage is evidently the dictate of nature; men and women were made to be companions of each other, and therefore I cannot be persuaded but that marriage is one of the means of happiness.'

'I know not,' said the princess, 'whether marriage be more than one of the innumerable modes of human misery. When I see and reckon the various forms of connubial infelicity, the unexpected causes of lasting discord, the diversities of temper, the oppositions of opinion, the rude collisions of contrary desire where both are urged by violent impulses, the obstinate contests of disagreeing virtues, where both are supported by conscious-ness of good intention, I am sometimes disposed to think with the severer casuists of most nations, that marriage is rather permitted than approved, and that none, but by the instigation of a passion too much indulged, entangle themselves with indissoluble compacts.'

'You seem to forget,' replied Rasselas, 'that you have, even now, represented celibacy as less happy than marriage. Both conditions may be bad, but they cannot both be worst. Thus it happens when wrong opinions are entertained, that they mutually destroy each other, and leave the mind open to truth.'

'I did not expect,' answered the princess, 'to hear that imputed to falsehood which is the consequence only of frailty. To the mind, as to the eye, it is difficult to compare with exactness objects vast in their extent, and various in their parts. Where we see or conceive the whole at once we readily note the discriminations and decide the preference: but of two systems, of which neither can be surveyed by any human being in its full compass of magnitude and multiplicity of complication, where is the wonder, that judging of the whole by parts, I am alternately affected by one and the other as either presses on my memory or fancy? We differ from ourselves just as we differ from each other, when we see only part of the question, as in the multifarious relations of politicks and morality: but when we perceive the whole at once, as in numerical computations, all agree in one judgment, and none ever varies his opinion.'

'Let us not add,' said the prince, 'to the other evils of life, the bitterness of controversy, nor endeavour to vie with each other in subtilties of argument. We are employed in a search, of which both are equally to enjoy the success, or suffer by the miscarriage. It is therefore fit that we assist each other. You surely conclude too hastily from the infelicity of marriage against its institution; will not the misery of life prove equally that life cannot be the gift of heaven? The world must be peopled by marriage, or peopled without it.'

'How the world is to be peopled,' returned Nekayah, 'is not my care, and needs not be yours. I see no danger that the present generation should omit to leave successors behind them: we are not now enquiring for the world, but for ourselves.'

CHAP. XXIX

The debate on marriage continued

'The good of the whole,' says Rasselas, 'is the same with the good of all its parts. If marriage be best for mankind it must be evidently best for individuals, or a permanent and necessary duty must be the cause of evil, and some must be inevitably sacrificed to the convenience of others. In the estimate which you have made of the two states, it appears that the incommodities of a single life are, in a great measure, necessary and certain, but those of the conjugal state accidental and avoidable.

'I cannot forbear to flatter myself that prudence and benevolence will make marriage happy. The general folly of mankind is the cause of general complaint. What can be expected but disappointment and repentance from a choice made in the immaturity of youth, in the ardour of desire, without judgment, without foresight, without enquiry after conformity of opinions, similarity of manners, rectitude of judgment, or purity of sentiment.

'Such is the common process of marriage. A youth and maiden meeting by chance, or brought together by artifice, exchange glances, reciprocate civilities, go home, and dream of one another. Having little to divert attention, or diversify thought, they find themselves uneasy when they are apart, and therefore conclude that they shall be happy together. They marry, and discover what nothing but voluntary blindness had before concealed; they wear out life in altercations, and charge nature with cruelty.

'From those early marriages proceeds likewise the rivalry of parents and children: the son is eager to enjoy the world before the father is willing to forsake it, and there is hardly room at once for two generations. The daughter begins to bloom before the mother can be content to fade, and neither can forbear to wish for the absence of the other.

'Surely all these evils may be avoided by that deliberation and delay which prudence prescribes to irrevocable choice. In the variety and jollity of youthful pleasures life may be well enough supported without the help of a partner. Longer time will increase experience, and wider views will allow better opportunities of enquiry and selection: one advantage, at least, will be certain; the parents will be visibly older than their children.'

'What reason cannot collect,'[1] said Nekayah, 'and what experiment has not yet taught, can be known only from the report of others. I have been told that late marriages are not eminently happy. This is a question too important to be neglected, and I have often proposed it to those, whose accuracy of remark, and comprehensiveness of knowledge, made their suffrages[2] worthy of regard. They have generally determined, that it is dangerous for a man and woman to suspend their fate upon each other, at a time when opinions are fixed, and habits are established; when friendships have been contracted on both sides, when life has been planned into method, and the mind has long enjoyed the contemplation of its own prospects.

'It is scarcely possible that two travelling through the world under the conduct of chance, should have been both directed to the same path, and it will not often happen that either will quit the track which custom has made pleasing. When the desultory levity of youth has settled into regularity, it is soon succeeded by pride ashamed to yield, or obstinacy delighting to contend. And even though mutual esteem produces mutual desire to please, time itself, as it modifies unchangeably the external mien, determines likewise the direction of the passions, and gives an inflexible rigidity to the manners. Long customs are not easily broken: he that attempts to change the course of his own life, very often labours in vain; and how shall we do that for others which we are seldom able to do for ourselves?'

'But surely,' interposed the prince, 'you suppose the chief motive of choice forgotten or neglected. Whenever I shall seek a wife, it shall be my first question, whether she be willing to be led by reason?'

'Thus it is,' said Nekayah, 'that philosophers are deceived. There are a thousand familiar disputes which reason never can decide; questions that elude investigation, and make logick ridiculous; cases where something must be done, and where little can be said. Consider the state of mankind, and enquire how few can be supposed to act upon any occasions, whether small or great, with all the reasons of action present to their minds. Wretched would be the pair above all names of wretchedness, who should be doomed to adjust by reason every morning all the minute detail of a domestick day.

'Those who marry at an advanced age, will probably escape the encroachments of their children; but, in diminution of this advantage, they will be likely to leave them, ignorant and helpless, to a guardian's mercy: or, if that should not happen, they must at least go out of the world before they see those whom they love best either wise or great.

'From their children, if they have less to fear, they have less also to hope, and they lose, without equivalent, the joys of early love, and the convenience of uniting with manners pliant, and minds susceptible of new impressions, which might wear away their dissimilitudes by long cohabitation, as soft bodies, by continual attrition, conform their surfaces to each other.

'I believe it will be found that those who marry late are best pleased with their children, and those who marry early with their partners.'

'The union of these two affections,' said Rasselas, 'would produce all that could be wished. Perhaps there is a time when marriage might unite them, a time neither too early for the father, nor too late for the husband.'

'Every hour,' answered the princess, 'confirms my prejudice in favour of the position so often uttered by the mouth of Imlac, "That nature sets her gifts on the right hand and on the left." Those conditions, which flatter hope and attract desire, are so constituted, that, as we approach one, we recede from another. There are goods so opposed that we cannot seize both, but, by too much prudence, may pass between them at too great a distance to reach either. This is often the fate of long consideration; he does nothing who endeavours to do more than is allowed to humanity. Flatter not yourself with contrarieties of pleasure. Of the blessings set before you make your choice, and be content. No man can taste the fruits of autumn while he is delighting his scent with the flowers of the spring: no man can, at the same time, fill his cup from the source and from the mouth of the Nile.'[3]

CHAP. XXX

Imlac enters, and changes the conversation

Here Imlac entered, and interrupted them. 'Imlac,' said Rasselas, 'I have been taking from the princess the dismal history of private life, and am almost discouraged from further search.'

'It seems to me,' said Imlac, 'that while you are making the choice of life, you neglect to live. You wander about a single

city, which, however large and diversified, can now afford few
novelties, and forget that you are in a country, famous among
the earliest monarchies for the power and wisdom of its inhabitants; a country where the sciences first dawned that illuminate
the world[1] and beyond which the arts cannot be traced of civil[2]
society or domestick life.

'The old Egyptians have left behind them monuments of
industry and power before which all European magnificence is
confessed to fade away. The ruins of their architecture are the
schools of modern builders, and from the wonders which time
has spared we may conjecture, though uncertainly, what it has
destroyed.'

'My curiosity,' said Rasselas, 'does not very strongly lead me
to survey piles of stone, or mounds of earth; my business is
with man. I came hither not to measure fragments of temples,
or trace choaked aqueducts, but to look upon the various scenes
of the present world.'[3]

'The things that are now before us,' said the princess, 'require
attention, and deserve it. What have I to do with the heroes or
the monuments of ancient times? with times which never can
return, and heroes, whose form of life was different from all
that the present condition of mankind requires or allows.'

'To know any thing,' returned the poet, 'we must know its
effects; to see men we must see their works, that we may learn
what reason has dictated, or passion has incited, and find what
are the most powerful motives of action. To judge rightly of
the present we must oppose it to the past; for all judgment is
comparative, and of the future nothing can be known. The
truth is, that no mind is much employed upon the present:
recollection and anticipation fill up almost all our moments.[4]
Our passions are joy and grief, love and hatred, hope and fear.[5]
Of joy and grief the past is the object, and the future of hope
and fear; even love and hatred respect the past, for the cause
must have been before the effect.

'The present state of things is the consequence of the former,
and it is natural to enquire what were the sources of the good
that we enjoy, or of the evil that we suffer. If we act only for
ourselves, to neglect the study of history is not prudent: if we

are entrusted with the care of others, it is not just. Ignorance, when it is voluntary, is criminal; and he may properly be charged with evil who refused to learn how he might prevent it.

'There is no part of history so generally useful as that which relates the progress of the human mind, the gradual improvement of reason, the successive advances of science, the vicissitudes of learning and ignorance, which are the light and darkness of thinking beings, the extinction and resuscitation of arts, and the revolutions of the intellectual world. If accounts of battles and invasions are peculiarly the business of princes, the useful or elegant arts are not to be neglected; those who have kingdoms to govern have understandings to cultivate.

'Example is always more efficacious than precept. A soldier is formed in war, and a painter must copy pictures. In this, contemplative life has the advantage: great actions are seldom seen, but the labours of art are always at hand for those who desire to know what art has been able to perform.

'When the eye or the imagination is struck with any uncommon work the next transition of an active mind is to the means by which it was performed. Here begins the true use of such contemplation; we enlarge our comprehension by new ideas, and perhaps recover some art lost to mankind, or learn what is less perfectly known in our own country. At least we compare our own with former times, and either rejoice at our improvements, or, what is the first motion towards good, discover our defects.'

'I am willing,' said the prince, 'to see all that can deserve my search.' 'And I,' said the princess, 'shall rejoice to learn something of the manners of antiquity.'

'The most pompous[6] monument of Egyptian greatness, and one of the most bulky works of manual industry,' said Imlac, 'are the pyramids; fabricks[7] raised before the time of history, and of which the earliest narratives afford us only uncertain traditions.[8] Of these the greatest is still standing very little injured by time.'

'Let us visit them to morrow,' said Nekayah. 'I have often heard of the pyramids, and shall not rest, till I have seen them within and without with my own eyes.'

CHAP. XXXI

They visit the pyramids

The resolution being thus taken, they set out the next day. They laid tents upon their camels, being resolved to stay among the pyramids till their curiosity was fully satisfied. They travelled gently, turned aside to every thing remarkable, stopped from time to time and conversed with the inhabitants, and observed the various appearances of towns ruined and inhabited, of wild and cultivated nature.

When they came to the great pyramid[1] they were astonished at the extent of the base, and the height of the top. Imlac explained to them the principles upon which the pyramidal form was chosen for a fabrick intended to co-extend its duration with that of the world: he shewed that its gradual diminution gave it such stability, as defeated all the common attacks of the elements, and could scarcely be overthrown by earthquakes themselves, the least resistible of natural violence. A concussion that should shatter the pyramid would threaten the dissolution of the continent.

They measured all its dimensions,[2] and pitched their tents at its foot. Next day they prepared to enter its interiour apartments, and having hired the common guides climbed up to the first passage, when the favourite of the princess, looking into the cavity, stepped back and trembled. 'Pekuah,' said the princess, 'of what art thou afraid?' 'Of the narrow entrance,' answered the lady, 'and of the dreadful gloom. I dare not enter a place which must surely be inhabited by unquiet souls. The original possessors of these dreadful vaults will start up before us, and, perhaps, shut us in for ever.' She spoke, and threw her arms round the neck of her mistress.

'If all your fear be of apparitions,' said the prince, 'I will promise you safety: there is no danger from the dead; he that is once buried will be seen no more.'

'That the dead are seen no more,' said Imlac, 'I will not undertake to maintain against the concurrent and unvaried testimony of all ages, and of all nations. There is no people, rude or learned, among whom apparitions of the dead are not related and believed. This opinion, which, perhaps, prevails as far as human nature is diffused, could become universal only by its truth: those, that never heard of one another, would not have agreed in a tale which nothing but experience can make credible. That it is doubted by single cavillers can very little weaken the general evidence, and some who deny it with their tongues confess it by their fears.

'Yet I do not mean to add new terrours to those which have already seized upon Pekuah. There can be no reason why spectres should haunt the pyramid more than other places, or why they should have power or will to hurt innocence and purity. Our entrance is no violation of their privileges; we can take nothing from them, how then can we offend them?'

'My dear Pekuah,' said the princess, 'I will always go before you, and Imlac shall follow you. Remember that you are the companion of the princess of Abissinia.'

'If the princess is pleased that her servant should die,' returned the lady, 'let her command some death less dreadful than enclosure in this horrid cavern. You know I dare not disobey you: I must go if you command me; but, if I once enter, I never shall come back.'

The princess saw that her fear was too strong for expostulation or reproof, and embracing her, told her that she should stay in the tent till their return. Pekuah was yet not satisfied, but entreated the princess not to persue so dreadful a purpose as that of entering the recesses of the pyramid. 'Though I cannot teach courage,' said Nekayah, 'I must not learn cowardice; nor leave at last undone what I came hither only to do.'

CHAP. XXXII

They enter the pyramid

Pekuah descended to the tents, and the rest entered the pyramid: they passed through the galleries, surveyed the vaults of marble, and examined the chest in which the body of the founder is supposed to have been reposited. They then sat down in one of the most spacious chambers to rest a while before they attempted to return.

'We have now,' said Imlac, 'gratified our minds with an exact view of the greatest work of man, except the wall of China.

'Of the wall it is very easy to assign the motives. It secured a wealthy and timorous nation from the incursions of barbarians, whose unskilfulness in arts made it easier for them to supply their wants by rapine than by industry, and who from time to time poured in upon the habitations of peaceful commerce, as vultures descend upon domestick fowl. Their celerity and fierceness made the wall necessary and their ignorance made it efficacious.

'But for the pyramids no reason has ever been given adequate to the cost and labour of the work. The narrowness of the chambers proves that it could afford no retreat from enemies, and treasures might have been reposited at far less expence with equal security. It seems to have been erected only in compliance with that hunger of imagination which preys incessantly upon life, and must be always appeased by some employment. Those who have already all that they can enjoy, must enlarge their desires.[1] He that has built for use, till use is supplied, must begin to build for vanity,[2] and extend his plan to the utmost power of human performance, that he may not be soon reduced to form another wish.

'I consider this mighty structure as a monument of the insufficiency of human enjoyments. A king, whose power is unlimited, and whose treasures surmount all real and imaginary wants, is compelled to solace, by the erection of a pyramid, the satiety of dominion and tastelesness of pleasures, and to amuse the tediousness of declining life, by seeing thousands labouring without end, and one stone, for no purpose, laid upon another. Whoever thou art, that, not content with a moderate condition, imaginest happiness in royal magnificence, and dreamest that command or riches can feed the appetite of novelty with perpetual gratifications, survey the pyramids, and confess thy folly!'

CHAP. XXXIII

The princess meets with an unexpected misfortune

They rose up, and returned through the cavity at which they had entered, and the princess prepared for her favourite a long narrative of dark labyrinths, and costly rooms, and of the different impressions which the varieties of the way had made upon her. But, when they came to their train, they found every one silent and dejected: the men discovered shame and fear in their countenances, and the women were weeping in the tents.

What had happened they did not try to conjecture, but immediately enquired. 'You had scarcely entered into the pyramid,' said one of the attendants, 'when a troop of Arabs rushed upon us: we were too few to resist them, and too slow to escape. They were about to search the tents, set us on our camels, and drive us along before them, when the approach of some Turkish horsemen put them to flight; but they seized the lady Pekuah with her two maids, and carried them away: the Turks are now persuing them by our instigation, but I fear they will not be able to overtake them.'[1]

The princess was overpowered with surprise and grief. Rasselas, in the first heat of his resentment, ordered his servants to follow him, and prepared to persue the robbers with his sabre in his hand. 'Sir,' said Imlac, 'what can you hope from violence or valour? the Arabs are mounted on horses trained to battle and retreat; we have only beasts of burthen. By leaving our present station we may lose the princess, but cannot hope to regain Pekuah.'

In a short time the Turks returned, having not been able to reach the enemy. The princess burst out into new lamentations, and Rasselas could scarcely forbear to reproach them with cowardice; but Imlac was of opinion, that the escape of the Arabs was no addition to their misfortune, for, perhaps, they would have killed their captives rather than have resigned them.

CHAP. XXXIV

They return to Cairo without Pekuah

There was nothing to be hoped from longer stay. They returned to Cairo repenting of their curiosity, censuring the negligence of the government, lamenting their own rashness which had neglected to procure a guard, imagining many expedients by which the loss of Pekuah might have been prevented, and resolving to do something for her recovery, though none could find any thing proper to be done.

Nekayah retired to her chamber, where her women attempted to comfort her, by telling her that all had their troubles, and that lady Pekuah had enjoyed much happiness in the world for a long time, and might reasonably expect a change of fortune. They hoped that some good would befal her wheresoever she was, and that their mistress would find another friend who might supply her place.

The princess made them no answer, and they continued the form of condolence, not much grieved in their hearts that the favourite was lost.

Next day the prince presented to the Bassa a memorial[1] of the wrong which he had suffered, and a petition for redress. The Bassa threatened to punish the robbers, but did not attempt to catch them, nor, indeed, could any account or description be given by which he might direct the persuit.

It soon appeared that nothing would be done by authority. Governours, being accustomed to hear of more crimes than they can punish, and more wrongs than they can redress, set themselves at ease by indiscriminate negligence, and presently forget the request when they lose sight of the petitioner.

Imlac then endeavoured to gain some intelligence by private agents. He found many who pretended to an exact knowledge of all the haunts of the Arabs, and to regular correspondence with their chiefs, and who readily undertook the recovery of Pekuah. Of these, some were furnished with money for their journey, and came back no more; some were liberally paid for accounts which a few days discovered to be false. But the princess would not suffer any means, however improbable, to be left untried. While she was doing something she kept her hope alive. As one expedient failed, another was suggested; when one messenger returned unsuccessful, another was despatched to a different quarter.

Two months had now passed, and of Pekuah nothing had been heard; the hopes which they had endeavoured to raise in each other grew more languid, and the princess, when she saw nothing more to be tried, sunk[2] down inconsolable in hopeless dejection. A thousand times she reproached herself with the easy compliance by which she permitted her favourite to stay behind her. 'Had not my fondness,' said she, 'lessened my authority, Pekuah had not dared to talk of her terrours. She ought to have feared me more than spectres. A severe look would have overpowered her; a peremptory command would have compelled obedience. Why did foolish indulgence prevail upon me? Why did I not speak and refuse to hear?'

'Great princess,' said Imlac, 'do not reproach yourself for your virtue, or consider that as blameable by which evil has accidentally been caused. Your tenderness for the timidity of Pekuah was generous and kind. When we act according to our duty, we commit the event to him by whose laws our actions are governed, and who will suffer none to be finally punished for obedience. When, in prospect of some good, whether natural or moral, we break the rules prescribed us, we withdraw from the direction of superior wisdom, and take all consequences upon ourselves. Man cannot so far know the connexion of causes and events, as that he may venture to do wrong in order to do right. When we persue our end by lawful means, we may always console our miscarriage by the hope of future recompense. When we consult only our own policy, and attempt to find a nearer way to good, by overleaping the settled boundaries of right and wrong, we cannot be happy even by success, because we cannot escape the consciousness of our fault; but, if we miscarry, the disappointment is irremediably embittered. How comfortless is the sorrow of him, who feels at once the pangs of guilt, and the vexation of calamity which guilt has brought upon him?

'Consider, princess, what would have been your condition, if the lady Pekuah had entreated to accompany you, and, being compelled to stay in the tents, had been carried away; or how would you have born the thought, if you had forced her into the pyramid, and she had died before you in agonies of terrour.'

'Had either happened,' said Nekayah, 'I could not have endured life till now: I should have been tortured to madness by the remembrance of such cruelty, or must have pined away in abhorrence of myself.'

'This at least,' said Imlac, 'is the present reward of virtuous conduct, that no unlucky consequence can oblige us to repent it.'

CHAP. XXXV

The princess languishes for want of Pekuah

Nekayah, being thus reconciled to herself, found that no evil is insupportable but that which is accompanied with consciousness of wrong. She was, from that time, delivered from the violence of tempestuous sorrow,[1] and sunk into silent pensiveness and gloomy tranquility. She sat from morning to evening recollecting all that had been done or said by her Pekuah, treasured up with care every trifle on which Pekuah had set an accidental value, and which might recal to mind any little incident or careless conversation. The sentiments of her, whom she now expected to see no more, were treasured in her memory as rules of life, and she deliberated to no other end than to conjecture on any occasion what would have been the opinion and counsel of Pekuah.

The women, by whom she was attended, knew nothing of her real condition,[2] and therefore she could not talk to them but with caution and reserve. She began to remit her curiosity, having no great care to collect notions which she had no convenience[3] of uttering. Rasselas endeavoured first to comfort and afterwards to divert her; he hired musicians, to whom she seemed to listen, but did not hear them, and procured masters to instruct her in various arts, whose lectures, when they visited her again, were again to be repeated. She had lost her taste of pleasure and her ambition of excellence. And her mind, though forced into short excursions, always recurred to the image of her friend.

Imlac was every morning earnestly enjoined to renew his enquiries, and was asked every night whether he had yet heard of Pekuah, till not being able to return the princess the answer that she desired, he was less and less willing to come into her presence. She observed his backwardness, and commanded him to attend her. 'You are not,' said she, 'to confound impatience with resentment, or to suppose that I charge you with negligence, because I repine at your unsuccessfulness. I do not much wonder at your absence; I know that the unhappy are never pleasing, and that all naturally avoid the contagion of misery. To hear complaints is wearisome alike to the wretched and the happy; for who would cloud by adventitious grief the short gleams of gaiety which life allows us? or who, that is struggling under his own evils, will add to them the miseries of another?

'The time is at hand, when none shall be disturbed any longer by the sighs of Nekayah: my search after happiness is now at an end. I am resolved to retire from the world with all its flatteries and deceits, and will hide myself in solitude, without any other care than to compose my thoughts, and regulate my hours by a constant succession of innocent occupations, till, with a mind purified from all earthly desires, I shall enter into that state, to which all are hastening, and in which I hope again to enjoy the friendship of Pekuah.'

'Do not entangle your mind,' said Imlac, 'by irrevocable

determinations, nor increase the burthen of life by a voluntary accumulation of misery: the weariness of retirement will continue or increase when the loss of Pekuah is forgotten. That you have been deprived of one pleasure is no very good reason for rejection of the rest.'

'Since Pekuah was taken from me,' said the princess, 'I have no pleasure to reject or to retain. She that has no one to love or trust has little to hope. She wants the radical[4] principle of happiness. We may, perhaps, allow that what satisfaction this world can afford, must arise from the conjunction of wealth, knowledge and goodness: wealth is nothing but as it is bestowed, and knowledge nothing but as it is communicated: they must therefore be imparted to others, and to whom could I now delight to impart them? Goodness affords the only comfort which can be enjoyed without a partner, and goodness may be practised in retirement.'

'How far solitude may admit goodness, or advance it, I shall not,' replied Imlac, 'dispute at present. Remember the confession of the pious hermit. You will wish to return into the world, when the image of your companion has left your thoughts.' 'That time,' said Nekayah, 'will never come. The generous frankness, the modest obsequiousness, and the faithful secrecy of my dear Pekuah, will always be more missed, as I shall live longer to see vice and folly.'

'The state of a mind oppressed with a sudden calamity,' said Imlac, 'is like that of the fabulous inhabitants of the new created earth, who, when the first night came upon them, supposed that day never would return. When the clouds of sorrow gather over us, we see nothing beyond them, nor can imagine how they will be dispelled: yet a new day succeeded to the night, and sorrow is never long without a dawn of ease. But they who restrain themselves from receiving comfort, do as the savages would have done, had they put out their eyes when it was dark. Our minds, like our bodies, are in continual flux; something is hourly lost, and something acquired. To lose much at once is inconvenient to either, but while the vital powers remain uninjured, nature will find the means of reparation. Distance has the same effect on the mind as on the eye, and while we glide along the stream of time, whatever we leave behind us is always lessening, and that which we approach increasing in magnitude. Do not suffer life to stagnate; it will grow muddy for want of motion:[5] commit yourself again to the current of the world; Pekuah will vanish by degrees; you will meet in your way some other favourite, or learn to diffuse[6] yourself in general conversation.'

'At least,' said the prince, 'do not despair before all remedies have been tried: the enquiry after the unfortunate lady is still continued, and shall be carried on with yet greater diligence, on condition that you will promise to wait a year for the event, without any unalterable resolution.'

Nekayah thought this a reasonable demand, and made the promise to her brother, who had been advised by Imlac to require it. Imlac had, indeed, no great hope of regaining Pekuah, but he supposed, that if he could secure the interval of a year, the princess would be then in no danger of a cloister.

CHAP. XXXVI

Pekuah is still remembered. The progress of sorrow

Nekayah, seeing that nothing was omitted for the recovery of her favourite, and having, by her promise, set her intention of retirement at a distance, began imperceptibly to return to common cares and common pleasures. She rejoiced without her own consent at the suspension of her sorrows, and sometimes caught herself with indignation in the act of turning away her mind from the remembrance of her, whom yet she resolved never to forget.

She then appointed a certain hour of the day for meditation on the merits and fondness of Pekuah, and for some weeks retired constantly at the time fixed, and returned with her eyes swollen and her countenance clouded. By degrees she grew less scrupulous, and suffered any important and pressing avocation[1] to delay the tribute of daily tears. She then yielded to less[2] occasions; sometimes forgot what she was indeed afraid to remember, and, at last, wholly released herself from the duty of periodical affliction.

Her real love of Pekuah was yet not diminished. A thousand occurrences brought her back to memory, and a thousand wants, which nothing but the confidence of friendship can supply, made her frequently regretted. She, therefore, solicited Imlac never to desist from enquiry, and to leave no art of intelligence untried, that, at least, she might have the comfort of knowing that she did not suffer by negligence or sluggishness. 'Yet what,' said she, 'is to be expected from our persuit of happiness, when we find the state of life to be such, that happiness itself is the cause of misery? Why should we endeavour to attain that, of which the possession cannot be secured? I shall henceforward fear to yield my heart to excellence, however bright, or to fondness, however tender, lest I should lose again what I have lost in Pekuah.'

CHAP. XXXVII

The princess hears news of Pekuah

In seven months, one of the messengers, who had been sent away upon the day when the promise was drawn from the princess, returned, after many unsuccessful rambles, from the borders of Nubia,[1] with an account that Pekuah was in the hands of an Arab chief, who possessed a castle or fortress on the extremity of Egypt. The Arab, whose revenue was plunder, was willing to restore her, with her two attendants, for two hundred ounces of gold.

The price was no subject of debate. The princess was in extasies when she heard that her favourite was alive, and might so cheaply be ransomed. She could not think of delaying for a moment Pekuah's happiness or her own, but entreated her brother to send back the messenger with the sum required. Imlac, being consulted, was not very confident of the veracity of the relator, and was still more doubtful of the Arab's faith, who might, if he were too liberally trusted, detain at once the money and the captives. He thought it dangerous to put themselves in the power of the Arab, by going into his district, and could not expect that the rover would so much expose himself as to come into the lower country, where he might be seized by the forces of the Bassa.

It is difficult to negotiate where neither will trust. But Imlac, after some deliberation, directed the messenger to propose that Pekuah should be conducted by ten horsemen to the monastery of St. Anthony, which is situated in the desarts of Upper-Egypt,[2] where she should be met by the same number, and her ransome should be paid.

That no time might be lost, as they expected that the proposal would not be refused, they immediately began their journey to the monastery; and, when they arrived, Imlac went forward with the former messenger to the Arab's fortress. Rasselas was desirous to go with them, but neither his sister nor Imlac would consent. The Arab, according to the custom of his nation, observed the laws of hospitality with great exactness to those who put themselves into his power, and, in a few days, brought Pekuah with her maids, by easy journeys, to their place appointed, where receiving the stipulated price, he restored her with great respect to liberty and her friends, and undertook to conduct them back towards Cairo beyond all danger of robbery or violence.

The princess and her favourite embraced each other with transport too violent to be expressed, and went out together to pour the tears of tenderness in secret, and exchange professions of kindness and gratitude. After a few hours they returned into the refectory of the convent, where, in the presence of the prior and his brethren, the prince required of Pekuah the history of her adventures.

CHAP. XXXVIII

The adventures of the lady Pekuah

'At what time, and in what manner, I was forced away,' said Pekuah, 'your servants have told you. The suddenness of the event struck me with surprise, and I was at first rather stupified than agitated with any passion of either fear or sorrow. My confusion was encreased by the speed and tumult of our flight while we were followed by the Turks, who, as it seemed, soon despaired to overtake us, or were afraid of those whom they made a shew of menacing.

'When the Arabs saw themselves out of danger they slackened their course, and, as I was less harrassed by external violence, I began to feel more uneasiness in my mind. After some time we stopped near a spring shaded with trees in a pleasant meadow, where we were set upon the ground, and offered such refreshments as our masters were partaking. I was suffered to sit with my maids apart from the rest, and none attempted to comfort or insult us. Here I first began to feel the full weight of my misery. The girls sat weeping in silence, and from time to time looked on me for succour. I knew not to what condition we were doomed, nor could conjecture where would be the place of our captivity, or whence to draw any hope of deliverance. I was in the hands of robbers and savages, and had no reason to suppose that their pity was more than their justice, or that they would forbear the gratification of any ardour of desire, or caprice of cruelty. I, however, kissed my maids, and endeavoured to pacify them by remarking, that we were yet treated with decency, and that, since we were now carried beyond persuit, there was no danger of violence to our lives.

'When we were to be set again on horseback, my maids clung round me, and refused to be parted, but I commanded them not to irritate those who had us in their power. We travelled the remaining part of the day through an unfrequented and pathless country, and came by moonlight to the side of a hill, where the rest of the troop was stationed. Their tents were pitched, and their fires kindled, and our chief was welcomed as a man much beloved by his dependants.

'We were received into a large tent, where we found women who had attended their husbands in the expedition. They set before us the supper which they had provided, and I eat it rather to encourage my maids than to comply with any appetite of my own. When the meat[1] was taken away they spread the carpets for repose. I was weary, and hoped to find in sleep that remission of distress which nature seldom denies. Ordering myself therefore to be undrest, I observed that the women looked very earnestly upon me, not expecting, I suppose, to see me so submissively attended. When my upper vest was taken off, they were apparently struck with the splendour of my cloaths, and one of them timorously laid her hand upon the embroidery. She then went out, and, in a short time, came back with another woman, who seemed to be of higher rank, and greater authority. She did, at her entrance, the usual act of reverence, and, taking me by the hand, placed me in a smaller tent, spread with finer carpets, where I spent the night quietly with my maids.

'In the morning, as I was sitting on the grass, the chief of the troop came towards me. I rose up to receive him, and he bowed with great respect. "Illustrious lady," said he, "my fortune is better than I had presumed to hope; I am told by my women, that I have a princess in my camp." "Sir," answered I, "your women have deceived themselves and you; I am not a princess, but an unhappy stranger who intended soon to have left this country, in which I am now to be imprisoned for ever." "Whoever, or whencesoever, you are," returned the Arab, "your dress, and that of your servants, shew your rank to be high, and your wealth to be great. Why should you, who can so easily procure your ransome, think yourself in danger of perpetual captivity? The purpose of my incursions is to encrease my riches, or more properly to gather tribute. The sons of Ishmael are the natural and hereditary lords of this part of the continent, which is usurped by late invaders, and low-born tyrants, from whom we are compelled to take by the sword what is denied to justice.[2] The violence of war admits no distinction; the lance that is lifted at guilt and power will sometimes fall on innocence and gentleness."

'"How little," said I, "did I expect that yesterday it should have fallen upon me."

'"Misfortunes," answered the Arab, "should always be expected. If the eye of hostility could learn reverence or pity, excellence like yours had been exempt from injury. But the angels of affliction spread their toils alike for the virtuous and the wicked, for the mighty and the mean. Do not be disconsolate; I am not one of the lawless and cruel rovers of the desert; I know the rules of civil life; I will fix your ransome, give a pasport to your messenger, and perform my stipulation with nice punctuality."[3]

'You will easily believe that I was pleased with his courtesy; and finding that his predominant passion was desire of money, I began now to think my danger less, for I knew that no sum would be thought too great for the release of Pekuah. I told him that he should have no reason to charge me with ingratitude, if I was used with kindness, and that any ransome, which could be expected for a maid of common rank, would be paid, but that he must not persist to rate me as a princess. He said, he would consider what he should demand, and then, smiling, bowed and retired.

'Soon after the women came about me, each contending to be more officious[4] than the other, and my maids themselves were served with reverence. We travelled onward by short journeys. On the fourth day the chief told me, that my ransome must be two hundred ounces of gold, which I not only promised him, but told him, that I would add fifty more, if I and my maids were honourably treated.

'I never knew the power of gold before. From that time I was the leader of the troop. The march of every day was longer or shorter as I commanded, and the tents were pitched where I chose to rest. We now had camels and other conveniencies for travel, my own women were always at my side, and I amused myself with observing the manners of the vagrant nations, and with viewing remains of ancient edifices with which these deserted countries appear to have been, in some distant age, lavishly embellished.

'The chief of the band was a man far from illiterate: he was able to travel by the stars or the compass, and had marked in his erratick expeditions such places as are most worthy the notice of a passenger.⁵ He observed to me, that buildings are always best preserved in places little frequented, and difficult of access: for, when once a country declines from its primitive splendour, the more inhabitants are left, the quicker ruin will be made. Walls supply stones more easily than quarries, and palaces and temples will be demolished to make stables of granate, and cottages of porphyry.

CHAP. XXXIX

The adventures of Pekuah continued

'We wandered about in this manner for some weeks, whether, as our chief pretended, for my gratification, or, as I rather suspected, for some convenience of his own. I endeavoured to appear contented where sullenness and resentment would have been of no use, and that endeavour conduced much to the calmness of my mind; but my heart was always with Nekayah, and the troubles of the night much overbalanced the amusements of the day. My women, who threw all their cares upon their mistress, set their minds at ease from the time when they saw me treated with respect, and gave themselves up to the incidental alleviations of our fatigue without solicitude or sorrow. I was pleased with their pleasure, and animated with their confidence. My condition had lost much of its terrour, since I found that the Arab ranged the country merely to get riches. Avarice is an uniform and tractable vice: other intellectual distempers are different in different constitutions of mind; that which sooths the pride of one will offend the pride of another; but to the favour of the covetous there is a ready way, bring money and nothing is denied.

'At last we came to the dwelling of our chief, a strong and spacious house built with stone in an island of the Nile, which lies, as I was told, under the tropick.[1] "Lady," said the Arab, "you shall rest after your journey a few weeks in this place, where you are to consider yourself as sovereign. My occupation is war: I have therefore chosen this obscure residence, from which I can issue unexpected, and to which I can retire unpersued. You may now repose in security: here are few pleasures, but here is no danger." He then led me into the inner apartments, and seating me on the richest couch, bowed to the ground. His women, who considered me as a rival, looked on me with malignity; but being soon informed that I was a great lady detained only for my ransome, they began to vie with each other in obsequiousness and reverence.

'Being again comforted with new assurances of speedy liberty, I was for some days diverted from impatience by the novelty of the place. The turrets overlooked the country to a great distance, and afforded a view of many windings of the stream. In the day I wandered from one place to another as the course of the sun varied the splendour of the prospect, and saw many things which I had never seen before. The crocodiles and river-horses[2] are common in this unpeopled region, and I often looked upon them with terrour, though I knew that they could not hurt me. For some time I expected to see mermaids and tritons, which, as Imlac has told me, the European travellers have stationed in the Nile, but no such beings ever appeared, and the Arab, when I enquired after them, laughed at my credulity.[3]

'At night the Arab always attended me to a tower set apart for celestial observations, where he endeavoured to teach me the names and courses of the stars. I had no great inclination to this study, but an appearance of attention was necessary to please my instructor, who valued himself for his skill, and, in a little while, I found some employment requisite to beguile the tediousness of time, which was to be passed always amidst the same objects. I was weary of looking in the morning on things from which I had turned away weary in the evening: I therefore was at last willing to observe the stars rather than do nothing, but could not always compose my thoughts, and was very often thinking on Nekayah when others imagined me contemplating the sky. Soon after the Arab went upon another expedition, and then my only pleasure was to talk with my maids about the accident by which we were carried away, and the happiness that we should all enjoy at the end of our captivity.'

'There were women in your Arab's fortress,' said the princess, 'why did you not make them your companions, enjoy their conversation, and partake their diversions? In a place where they found business or amusement, why should you alone sit corroded with idle melancholy? or why could not you bear for a few months that condition to which they were condemned for life?'

'The diversions of the women,' answered Pekuah, 'were only childish play, by which the mind accustomed to stronger operations could not be kept busy. I could do all which they delighted in doing by powers merely sensitive,[4] while my intellectual faculties were flown to Cairo. They ran from room to room as a bird hops from wire to wire in his cage. They danced for the sake of motion, as lambs frisk in a meadow. One sometimes pretended to be hurt that the rest might be alarmed, or hid herself that another might seek her. Part of their time passed in watching the progress of light bodies that floated on the river, and part in marking the various forms into which clouds broke in the sky.

'Their business was only needlework, in which I and my maids sometimes helped them; but you know that the mind will easily straggle from the fingers, nor will you suspect that captivity and absence from Nekayah could receive solace from silken flowers.

'Nor was much satisfaction to be hoped from their conversation: for of what could they be expected to talk? They had seen nothing; for they had lived from early youth in that narrow spot: of what they had not seen they could have no knowledge, for they could not read. They had no ideas but of the few things that were within their view, and had hardly names for any thing but their cloaths and their food. As I bore a superiour character, I was often called to terminate their quarrels, which I decided as equitably as I could. If it could have amused me to hear the complaints of each against the rest, I might have been often detained by long stories, but the motives of their animosity were so small that I could not listen without intercepting[5] the tale.'

'How,' said Rasselas, 'can the Arab, whom you represented as a man of more than common accomplishments, take any pleasure in his seraglio, when it is filled only with women like these. Are they exquisitely beautiful?'

'They do not,' said Pekuah, 'want that unaffecting and ignoble beauty which may subsist without spriteliness or sublimity, without energy of thought or dignity of virtue. But to a man like the Arab such beauty was only a flower casually plucked and carelesly thrown away. Whatever pleasures he might find among them, they were not those of friendship or society. When they were playing about him he looked on them with inattentive superiority: when they vied for his regard he sometimes turned away disgusted. As they had no knowledge, their talk could take nothing from the tediousness of life: as they had no choice, their fondness, or appearance of fondness, excited in him neither pride nor gratitude; he was not exalted in his own esteem by the smiles of a woman who saw no other man, nor was much obliged by that regard, of which he could never know the sincerity, and which he might often perceive to be exerted not so much to delight him as to pain a rival. That which he gave, and they received, as love, was only a careless distribution of superfluous time, such love as man can bestow upon that which he despises, such as has neither hope nor fear, neither joy nor sorrow.'

'You have reason, lady, to think yourself happy,' said Imlac, 'that you have been thus easily dismissed. How could a mind, hungry for knowledge, be willing, in an intellectual famine, to lose such a banquet as Pekuah's conversation?'

'I am inclined to believe,' answered Pekuah, 'that he was for some time in suspense; for, notwithstanding his promise, whenever I proposed to despatch a messenger to Cairo, he found some excuse for delay. While I was detained in his house he made many incursions into the neighbouring countries, and, perhaps, he would have refused to discharge me, had his plunder been equal to his wishes. He returned always courteous, related his adventures, delighted to hear my observations, and endeavoured to advance my acquaintance with the stars. When I importuned him to send away my letters, he soothed me with professions of honour and sincerity; and, when I could be no longer decently denied, put his troop again in motion, and left me to govern in his absence. I was much afflicted by this studied procrastination, and was sometimes afraid that I should be forgotten; that you would leave Cairo, and I must end my days in an island of the Nile.

'I grew at last hopeless and dejected, and cared so little to entertain him, that he for a while more frequently talked with my maids. That he should fall in love with them, or with me, might have been equally fatal, and I was not much pleased with the growing friendship. My anxiety was not long; for, as I recovered some degree of chearfulness, he returned to me, and I could not forbear to despise my former uneasiness.

'He still delayed to send for my ransome, and would, perhaps, never have determined, had not your agent found his way to him. The gold, which he would not fetch, he could not reject when it was offered. He hastened to prepare for our journey hither, like a man delivered from the pain of an intestine conflict. I took leave of my companions in the house, who dismissed me with cold indifference.'

Nekayah, having heard her favourite's relation, rose and embraced her, and Rasselas gave her an hundred ounces of gold, which she presented to the Arab for the fifty that were promised.

CHAP. XL

The history of a man of learning

They returned to Cairo, and were so well pleased at finding themselves together, that none of them went much abroad. The prince began to love learning, and one day declared to Imlac, that he intended to devote himself to science, and pass the rest of his days in literary solitude.

'Before you make your final choice,' answered Imlac, 'you ought to examine its hazards, and converse with some of those who are grown old in the company of themselves. I have just left the observatory of one of the most learned astronomers in the world, who has spent forty years in unwearied attention to the motions and appearances of the celestial bodies, and has drawn out his soul in endless calculations. He admits a few friends once a month to hear his deductions and enjoy his discoveries. I was introduced as a man of knowledge worthy of his notice. Men of various ideas and fluent conversation are commonly welcome to those whose thoughts have been long fixed upon a single point, and who find the images of other things stealing away. I delighted him with my remarks, he smiled at the narrative of my travels, and was glad to forget the constellations, and descend for a moment into the lower world.

'On the next day of vacation[1] I renewed my visit, and was so fortunate as to please him again. He relaxed from that time the severity of his rule, and permitted me to enter at my own choice. I found him always busy, and always glad to be relieved. As each knew much which the other was desirous of learning, we exchanged our notions with great delight. I perceived that I had every day more of his confidence, and always found new cause of admiration in the profundity of his mind. His comprehension is vast, his memory capacious and retentive, his discourse is methodical, and his expression clear.

'His integrity and benevolence are equal to his learning. His deepest researches and most favourite studies are willingly interrupted for any opportunity of doing good by his counsel or his riches. To his closest retreat, at his most busy moments, all are admitted that want his assistance: "For though I exclude idleness and pleasure, I will never," says he, "bar my doors against charity. To man is permitted the contemplation of the skies, but the practice of virtue is commanded."'

'Surely,' said the princess, 'this man is happy.'

'I visited him,' said Imlac, 'with more and more frequency, and was every time more enamoured of his conversation: he was sublime² without haughtiness, courteous without formality, and communicative without ostentation. I was at first, great princess, of your opinion, thought him the happiest of mankind, and often congratulated him on the blessing that he enjoyed. He seemed to hear nothing with indifference but the praises of his condition, to which he always returned a general answer, and diverted the conversation to some other topick.

'Amidst this willingness to be pleased, and labour to please, I had quickly reason to imagine that some painful sentiment pressed upon his mind. He often looked up earnestly towards the sun, and let his voice fall in the midst of his discourse. He would sometimes, when we were alone, gaze upon me in silence with the air of a man who longed to speak what he was yet resolved to suppress. He would often send for me with vehement injunctions of haste, though, when I came to him, he had nothing extraordinary to say. And sometimes, when I was leaving him, would call me back, pause a few moments and then dismiss me.

CHAP. XLI

The astronomer discovers¹ the cause of his uneasiness

'At last the time came when the secret burst his reserve. We were sitting together last night in the turret of his house, watching the emersion² of a satellite of Jupiter. A sudden tempest clouded the sky, and disappointed our observation. We sat a while silent in the dark, and then he addressed himself to me in these words: "Imlac, I have long considered thy friendship as the greatest blessing of my life. Integrity without knowledge is weak and useless, and knowledge without integrity is dangerous and dreadful. I have found in thee all the qualities requisite for trust, benevolence, experience, and fortitude. I have long discharged an office which I must soon quit at the call of nature, and shall rejoice in the hour of imbecility and pain to devolve it upon thee."

'I thought myself honoured by this testimony, and protested that whatever could conduce to his happiness would add likewise to mine.

' "Hear, Imlac, what thou wilt not without difficulty credit. I have possessed for five years the regulation of weather, and the distribution of the seasons: the sun has listened to my dictates, and passed from tropick to tropick by my direction; the clouds, at my call, have poured their waters, and the Nile has overflowed at my command; I have restrained the rage of the dog-star, and mitigated the fervours of the crab.³ The winds alone, of all the elemental⁴ powers, have hitherto refused my authority, and multitudes have perished by equinoctial tempests which I found myself unable to prohibit or restrain. I have administered this great office with exact justice, and made to the different nations of the earth an impartial dividend of rain and sunshine. What must have been the misery of half the globe, if I had limited the clouds to particular regions, or confined the sun to either side of the equator?"

CHAP. XLII

The opinion of the astronomer is explained and justified

'I suppose he discovered in me, through the obscurity of the room, some tokens of amazement and doubt, for, after a short pause, he proceeded thus:

'"Not to be easily credited will neither surprise nor offend me; for I am, probably, the first of human beings to whom this trust has been imparted. Nor do I know whether to deem this distinction a reward or punishment; since I have possessed it I have been far less happy than before, and nothing but the consciousness of good intention could have enabled me to support the weariness of unremitted vigilance."

'"How long, Sir," said I, "has this great office been in your hands?"

'"About ten years ago," said he, "my daily observations of the changes of the sky led me to consider, whether, if I had the power of the seasons, I could confer greater plenty upon the inhabitants of the earth. This contemplation fastened on my mind, and I sat days and nights in imaginary dominion, pouring upon this country and that the showers of fertility, and seconding every fall of rain with a due proportion of sunshine. I had yet only the will to do good, and did not imagine that I should ever have the power.

'"One day as I was looking on the fields withering with heat, I felt in my mind a sudden wish that I could send rain on the southern mountains, and raise the Nile to an inundation.¹ In the hurry of my imagination I commanded rain to fall, and, by comparing the time of my command, with that of the inundation, I found that the clouds had listned to my lips."

'"Might not some other cause," said I, "produce this concurrence? the Nile does not always rise on the same day."

'"Do not believe," said he with impatience, "that such objections could escape me: I reasoned long against my own conviction, and laboured against truth with the utmost obstinacy. I sometimes suspected myself of madness, and should not have dared to impart this secret but to a man like you, capable of distinguishing the wonderful from the impossible, and the incredible from the false."

'"Why, Sir," said I, "do you call that incredible, which you know, or think you know, to be true."

'"Because," said he, "I cannot prove it by any external evidence; and I know too well the laws of demonstration to think that my conviction ought to influence another, who cannot, like me, be conscious of its force. I, therefore, shall not attempt to gain credit by disputation. It is sufficient that I feel this power, that I have long possessed, and every day exerted it. But the life of man is short, the infirmities of age increase upon me, and the time will soon come when the regulator of the year must mingle with the dust. The care of appointing a successor has long disturbed me; the night and the day have been spent in comparisons of all the characters which have come to my knowledge, and I have yet found none so worthy as thyself.

CHAP. XLIII

The astronomer leaves Imlac his directions

' "Hear therefore, what I shall impart, with attention, such as the welfare of a world requires. If the task of a king be considered as difficult, who has the care only of a few millions, to whom he cannot do much good or harm, what must be the anxiety of him, on whom depend the action of the elements, and the great gifts of light and heat!—Hear me therefore with attention.

' "I have diligently considered the position of the earth and sun, and formed innumerable schemes in which I changed their situation. I have sometimes turned aside the axis of the earth, and sometimes varied the ecliptick of the sun: but I have found it impossible to make a disposition by which the world may be advantaged; what one region gains, another loses by any imaginable alteration, even without considering the distant parts of the solar system with which we are unacquainted. Do not, therefore, in thy administration of the year, indulge thy pride by innovation; do not please thyself with thinking that thou canst make thyself renowned to all future ages, by disordering the seasons. The memory of mischief is no desirable fame. Much less will it become thee to let kindness or interest prevail. Never rob other countries of rain to pour it on thine own. For us the Nile is sufficient."

'I promised that when I possessed the power, I would use it with inflexible integrity, and he dismissed me, pressing my hand. "My heart," said he, "will be now at rest, and my benevolence will no more destroy my quiet: I have found a man of wisdom and virtue, to whom I can chearfully bequeath the inheritance of the sun."'

The prince heard this narration with very serious regard, but the princess smiled, and Pekuah convulsed herself with laughter. 'Ladies,' said Imlac, 'to mock the heaviest of human afflictions is neither charitable nor wise. Few can attain this man's knowledge, and few practise his virtues; but all may suffer his calamity. Of the uncertainties of our present state, the most dreadful and alarming is the uncertain continuance of reason.'[1]

The princess was recollected,[2] and the favourite was abashed. Rasselas, more deeply affected, enquired of Imlac, whether he thought such maladies of the mind frequent, and how they were contracted.

CHAP. XLIV

The dangerous prevalence[1] of imagination

'Disorders of intellect,' answered Imlac, 'happen much more often than superficial observers will easily believe. Perhaps, if we speak with rigorous exactness, no human mind is in its right state. There is no man whose imagination does not sometimes predominate over his reason, who can regulate his attention wholly by his will, and whose ideas will come and go at his command. No man will be found in whose mind airy[2] notions do not sometimes tyrannise, and force him to hope or fear beyond the limits of sober probability. All power of fancy over reason is a degree of insanity; but while this power is such as we can controll and repress, it is not visible to others, nor considered as any depravation of the mental faculties: it is not pronounced madness but when it comes ungovernable, and apparently influences speech or action.

'To indulge the power of fiction, and send imagination out upon the wing, is often the sport of those who delight too much in silent speculation. When we are alone we are not always busy; the labour of excogitation is too violent to last long; the ardour of enquiry will sometimes give way to idleness or satiety. He who has nothing external that can divert him, must find pleasure in his own thoughts, and must conceive himself what he is not; for who is pleased with what he is? He then expatiates in boundless futurity, and culls from all imaginable conditions that which for the present moment he should most desire, amuses his desires with impossible enjoyments, and confers upon his pride unattainable dominion.[3] The mind dances from scene to scene, unites all pleasures in all combinations, and riots in delights which nature and fortune, with all their bounty, cannot bestow.

'In time some particular train of ideas fixes the attention, all other intellectual gratifications are rejected, the mind, in weariness or leisure, recurs constantly to the favourite conception, and feasts on the luscious[4] falsehood whenever she is offended with the bitterness of truth. By degrees the reign of fancy is confirmed; she grows first imperious, and in time despotick. Then fictions begin to operate as realities, false opinions fasten upon the mind, and life passes in dreams of rapture or of anguish.

'This, Sir, is one of the dangers of solitude, which the hermit has confessed not always to promote goodness, and the astronomer's misery has proved to be not always propitious to wisdom.'

'I will no more,' said the favourite, 'imagine myself the queen of Abissinia. I have often spent the hours, which the princess gave to my own disposal, in adjusting ceremonies and regulating the court; I have repressed the pride of the powerful, and granted the petitions of the poor; I have built new palaces in more happy situations, planted groves upon the tops of mountains, and have exulted in the beneficence of royalty, till, when the princess entered, I had almost forgotten to bow down before her.'

'And I,' said the princess, 'will not allow myself any more to

play the shepherdess in my waking dreams. I have often soothed
my thoughts with the quiet and innocence of pastoral employments, till I have in my chamber heard the winds whistle, and
the sheep bleat; sometimes freed the lamb entangled in the
thicket, and sometimes with my crook encountered the wolf. I
have a dress like that of the village maids, which I put on to
help my imagination, and a pipe on which I play softly, and
suppose myself followed by my flocks.'

'I will confess,' said the prince, 'an indulgence of fantastick[5]
delight more dangerous than yours. I have frequently endeavoured to image the possibility of a perfect government, by which
all wrong should be restrained, all vice reformed, and all the
subjects preserved in tranquility and innocence. This thought
produced innumerable schemes of reformation, and dictated
many useful regulations and salutary edicts. This has been the
sport and sometimes the labour of my solitude; and I start,
when I think with how little anguish I once supposed the death
of my father and my brothers.'

'Such,' says Imlac, 'are the effects of visionary schemes: when
we first form them we know them to be absurd, but familiarise
them by degrees, and in time lose sight of their folly.'

CHAP. XLV

They discourse with an old man

The evening was now far past, and they rose to return home.
As they walked along the bank of the Nile, delighted with the
beams of the moon quivering on the water, they saw at a small
distance an old man, whom the prince had often heard in the
assembly of the sages. 'Yonder,' said he, 'is one whose years
have calmed his passions, but not clouded his reason: let us
close the disquisitions of the night, by enquiring what are his
sentiments of his own state, that we may know whether youth
alone is to struggle with vexation, and whether any better hope
remains for the latter part of life.'

Here the sage approached and saluted them. They invited him to join their walk, and prattled[1] a while as acquaintance that had unexpectedly met one another. The old man was chearful and talkative, and the way seemed short in his company. He was pleased to find himself not disregarded, accompanied them to their house, and, at the prince's request, entered with them. They placed him in the seat of honour, and set wine and conserves before him.

'Sir,' said the princess, 'an evening walk must give to a man of learning, like you, pleasures which ignorance and youth can hardly conceive. You know the qualities and the causes of all that you behold, the laws by which the river flows, the periods in which the planets perform their revolutions. Every thing must supply you with contemplation, and renew the consciousness of your own dignity.'

'Lady,' answered he, 'let the gay and the vigorous expect pleasure in their excursions, it is enough that age can obtain ease. To me the world has lost its novelty: I look round, and see what I remember to have seen in happier days. I rest against a tree, and consider, that in the same shade I once disputed upon the annual overflow of the Nile with a friend who is now silent in the grave. I cast my eyes upwards, fix them on the changing moon, and think with pain on the vicissitudes of life. I have ceased to take much delight in physical[2] truth; for what have I to do with those things which I am soon to leave?'

'You may at least recreate[3] yourself,' said Imlac, 'with the recollection of an honourable and useful life, and enjoy the praise which all agree to give you.'

'Praise,' said the sage, with a sigh, 'is to an old man an empty sound. I have neither mother to be delighted with the reputation of her son, nor wife to partake the honours of her husband. I have outlived my friends and my rivals. Nothing is now of much importance; for I cannot extend my interest beyond myself.[4] Youth is delighted with applause, because it is considered as the earnest of some future good, and because the prospect of life is far extended: but to me, who am now declining to decrepitude, there is little to be feared from the malevolence of men, and yet less to be hoped from their affection or esteem.

Something they may yet take away, but they can give me nothing. Riches would now be useless, and high employment would be pain. My retrospect of life recalls to my view many opportunities of good neglected, much time squandered upon trifles, and more lost in idleness and vacancy.[5] I leave many great designs unattempted, and many great attempts unfinished. My mind is burthened with no heavy crime, and therefore I compose myself to tranquility; endeavour to abstract my thoughts from hopes and cares, which, though reason knows them to be vain, still try to keep their old possession of the heart; expect, with serene humility, that hour which nature cannot long delay; and hope to possess in a better state that happiness which here I could not find, and that virtue which here I have not attained.'

He rose and went away, leaving his audience not much elated with the hope of long life. The prince consoled himself with remarking, that it was not reasonable to be disappointed by this account; for age had never been considered as the season of felicity, and, if it was possible to be easy in decline and weakness, it was likely that the days of vigour and alacrity might be happy; that the noon of life might be bright, if the evening could be calm.

The princess suspected that age was querulous and malignant, and delighted to repress the expectations of those who had newly entered the world. She had seen the possessors of estates look with envy on their heirs, and known many who enjoy pleasure no longer than they can confine it to themselves.

Pekuah conjectured, that the man was older than he appeared, and was willing to impute his complaints to delirious dejection; or else supposed that he had been unfortunate, and was therefore discontented: 'For nothing,' said she, 'is more common than to call our own condition, the condition of life.'

Imlac, who had no desire to see them depressed, smiled at the comforts which they could so readily procure to themselves, and remembered, that at the same age, he was equally confident of unmingled prosperity, and equally fertile of consolatory expedients. He forbore to force upon them unwelcome knowledge, which time itself would too soon impress. The princess and her lady retired; the madness of the astronomer hung upon their minds, and they desired Imlac to enter upon his office, and delay next morning the rising of the sun.

CHAP. XLVI

The princess and Pekuah visit the astronomer

The princess and Pekuah having talked in private of Imlac's astronomer, thought his character at once so amiable and so strange, that they could not be satisfied without a nearer knowledge, and Imlac was requested to find the means of bringing them together.

This was somewhat difficult; the philosopher had never received any visits from women, though he lived in a city that had in it many Europeans who followed the manners of their own countries, and many from other parts of the world that lived there with European liberty. The ladies would not be refused, and several schemes were proposed for the accomplishment of their design. It was proposed to introduce them as strangers in distress, to whom the sage was always accessible; but, after some deliberation, it appeared, that by this artifice, no acquaintance could be formed, for their conversation would be short, and they could not decently importune him often. 'This,' said Rasselas, 'is true; but I have yet a stronger objection against the misrepresentation of your state. I have always considered it as treason against the great republick of human nature, to make any man's virtues the means of deceiving him, whether on great or little occasions. All imposture weakens confidence and chills benevolence. When the sage finds that you are not what you seemed, he will feel the resentment natural to a man who, conscious of great abilities, discovers that he has been tricked by understandings meaner than his own, and, perhaps, the distrust, which he can never afterwards wholly lay aside, may stop the voice of counsel, and close the hand of charity; and where will you find the power of restoring his benefactions to mankind, or his peace to himself?'

To this no reply was attempted, and Imlac began to hope that their curiosity would subside; but, next day, Pekuah told him, she had now found an honest pretence for a visit to the astronomer, for she would solicit permission to continue under him the studies in which she had been initiated by the Arab, and the princess might go with her either as a fellow-student, or because a woman could not decently come alone. 'I am afraid,' said Imlac, 'that he will be soon weary of your company: men advanced far in knowledge do not love to repeat the elements of their art, and I am not certain, that even of the elements, as he will deliver them connected with inferences, and mingled with reflections, you are a very capable auditress.' 'That,' said Pekuah, 'must be my care: I ask of you only to take me thither. My knowledge is, perhaps, more than you imagine it, and by concurring always with his opinions I shall make him think it greater than it is.'

The astronomer, in pursuance of this resolution, was told, that a foreign lady, travelling in search of knowledge, had heard of his reputation, and was desirous to become his scholar. The uncommonness of the proposal raised at once his surprise and curiosity, and when, after a short deliberation, he consented to admit her, he could not stay[1] without impatience till the next day.

The ladies dressed themselves magnificently, and were attended by Imlac to the astronomer, who was pleased to see himself approached with respect by persons of so splendid an appearance. In the exchange of the first civilities he was timorous and bashful; but, when the talk became regular, he recollected his powers, and justified the character which Imlac had given. Enquiring of Pekuah what could have turned her inclination towards astronomy, he received from her a history of her adventure at the pyramid, and of the time passed in the Arab's island. She told her tale with ease and elegance, and her conversation took possession of his heart. The discourse was then turned to astronomy: Pekuah displayed what she knew: he looked upon her as a prodigy of genius, and entreated her not to desist from a study which she had so happily begun.

They came again and again, and were every time more welcome than before. The sage endeavoured to amuse them, that they might prolong their visits, for he found his thoughts grow brighter in their company; the clouds of solicitude vanished by degrees, as he forced himself to entertain them, and he grieved when he was left at their departure to his old employment of regulating the seasons.

The princess and her favourite had now watched his lips for several months, and could not catch a single word from which they could judge whether he continued, or not, in the opinion of his preternatural commission. They often contrived to bring him to an open declaration, but he easily eluded all their attacks, and on which side soever they pressed him escaped from them to some other topick.

As their familiarity increased they invited him often to the house of Imlac, where they distinguished him by extraordinary respect. He began gradually to delight in sublunary pleasures. He came early and departed late; laboured to recommend himself by assiduity and compliance; excited their curiosity after new arts, that they might still want his assistance; and when they made any excursion of pleasure or enquiry, entreated to attend them.

By long experience of his integrity and wisdom, the prince and his sister were convinced that he might be trusted without danger; and, lest he should draw any false hopes from the civilities which he received, discovered to him their condition, with the motives of their journey, and required his opinion on the choice of life.

'Of the various conditions which the world spreads before you, which you shall prefer,' said the sage, 'I am not able to instruct you. I can only tell that I have chosen wrong. I have passed my time in study without experience; in the attainment of sciences which can, for the most part, be but remotely useful to mankind. I have purchased knowledge at the expence of all the common comforts of life: I have missed the endearing elegance of female friendship, and the happy commerce[2] of domestick tenderness. If I have obtained any prerogatives above other students, they have been accompanied with fear, disquiet, and scrupulosity;[3] but even of these prerogatives, whatever they were, I have, since my thoughts have been diversified by more intercourse with the world, begun to question the reality. When I have been for a few days lost in pleasing dissipation, I am always tempted to think that my enquiries have ended in errour, and that I have suffered much, and suffered it in vain.'

Imlac was delighted to find that the sage's understanding was breaking through its mists, and resolved to detain him from the planets till he should forget his task of ruling them, and reason should recover its original influence.

From this time the astronomer was received into familiar friendship, and partook of all their projects and pleasures: his respect kept him attentive, and the activity of Rasselas did not leave much time unengaged. Something was always to be done; the day was spent in making observations which furnished talk for the evening, and the evening was closed with a scheme for the morrow.

The sage confessed to Imlac, that since he had mingled in the gay tumults of life, and divided his hours by a succession of amusements, he found the conviction of his authority over the skies fade gradually from his mind, and began to trust less to an opinion which he never could prove to others, and which he now found subject to variation from causes in which reason had no part. 'If I am accidentally left alone for a few hours,' said he, 'my inveterate persuasion rushes upon my soul, and my thoughts are chained down by some irresistible violence, but they are soon disentangled by the prince's conversation, and instantaneously released at the entrance of Pekuah. I am like a man habitually afraid of spectres, who is set at ease by a lamp, and wonders at the dread which harrassed him in the dark, yet, if his lamp be extinguished, feels again the terrours which he knows that when it is light he shall feel no more. But I am sometimes afraid lest I indulge my quiet by criminal negligence, and voluntarily forget the great charge with which I am intrusted. If I favour myself in a known errour, or am determined by my own ease in a doubtful question of this importance, how dreadful is my crime!'

'No disease of the imagination,' answered Imlac, 'is so difficult of cure, as that which is complicated with the dread of guilt: fancy and conscience then act interchangeably upon us, and so often shift their places, that the illusions of one are not distinguished from the dictates of the other. If fancy presents images not moral or religious, the mind drives them away when they give it pain, but when melancholick notions take the form of duty, they lay hold on the faculties without opposition, because we are afraid to exclude or banish them. For this reason the superstitious are often melancholy, and the melancholy almost always superstitious.

'But do not let the suggestions of timidity overpower your better reason: the danger of neglect can be but as the probability of the obligation, which, when you consider it with freedom, you find very little, and that little growing every day less. Open your heart to the influence of the light, which, from time to time, breaks in upon you: when scruples importune you, which you in your lucid moments know to be vain, do not stand to parley, but fly to business or to Pekuah, and keep this thought always prevalent, that you are only one atom of the mass of humanity, and have neither such virtue nor vice, as that you should be singled out for supernatural favours or afflictions.'

CHAP. XLVII

The prince enters, and brings a new topick

'All this,' said the astronomer, 'I have often thought, but my reason has been so long subjugated by an uncontrolable and overwhelming idea, that it durst not confide in its own decisions. I now see how fatally I betrayed my quiet, by suffering chimeras to prey upon me in secret; but melancholy shrinks from communication, and I never found a man before, to whom I could impart my troubles, though I had been certain of relief. I rejoice to find my own sentiments confirmed by yours, who are not easily deceived, and can have no motive or purpose to deceive. I hope that time and variety will dissipate the gloom that has so long surrounded me, and the latter part of my days will be spent in peace.'

'Your learning and virtue,' said Imlac, 'may justly give you hopes.'

Rasselas then entered with the princess and Pekuah, and enquired whether they had contrived any new diversion for the next day. 'Such,' said Nekayah, 'is the state of life, that none are happy but by the anticipation of change: the change itself is nothing; when we have made it, the next wish is to change again. The world is not yet exhausted; let me see something to morrow which I never saw before.'

'Variety,' said Rasselas, 'is so necessary to content,[1] that even the Happy Valley disgusted me by the recurrence of its luxuries; yet I could not forbear to reproach myself with impatience, when I saw the monks of St. Anthony support without complaint, a life, not of uniform delight, but uniform hardship.'

'Those men,' answered Imlac, 'are less wretched in their silent convent than the Abissinian princes in their prison of pleasure. Whatever is done by the monks is incited by an adequate and reasonable motive. Their labour supplies them with necessaries; it therefore cannot be omitted, and is certainly rewarded. Their devotion prepares them for another state, and reminds them of its approach, while it fits them for it. Their time is regularly distributed; one duty succeeds another, so that they are not left open to the distraction of unguided choice, nor lost in the shades of listless inactivity. There is a certain task to be performed at an appropriated hour; and their toils are cheerful, because they consider them as acts of piety, by which they are always advancing towards endless felicity.'

'Do you think,' said Nekayah, 'that the monastick rule is a more holy and less imperfect state than any other? May not he equally hope for future happiness who converses[2] openly with mankind, who succours the distressed by his charity, instructs the ignorant by his learning, and contributes by his industry to the general system of life; even though he should omit some of the mortifications which are practised in the cloister, and allow himself such harmless delights as his condition may place within his reach?'

'This,' said Imlac, 'is a question which has long divided the wise, and perplexed the good. I am afraid to decide on either part. He that lives well in the world is better than he that lives well in a monastery. But, perhaps, every one is not able to stem the temptations of publick life; and, if he cannot conquer, he may properly retreat. Some have little power to do good, and have likewise little strength to resist evil. Many are weary of their conflicts with adversity, and are willing to eject those passions which have long busied them in vain. And many are dismissed by age and diseases from the more laborious duties of society. In monasteries the weak and timorous may be happily sheltered, the weary may repose, and the penitent may meditate. Those retreats of prayer and contemplation have something so congenial to the mind of man, that, perhaps, there is scarcely one that does not purpose to close his life in pious abstraction with a few associates serious as himself.'

'Such,' said Pekuah, 'has often been my wish, and I have heard the princess declare, that she should not willingly die in a croud.'

'The liberty of using harmless pleasures,' proceeded Imlac, 'will not be disputed; but it is still to be examined what pleasures are harmless. The evil of any pleasure that Nekayah can image is not in the act itself, but in its consequences. Pleasure, in itself harmless, may become mischievous, by endearing to us a state which we know to be transient and probatory,[3] and with-drawing our thoughts from that, of which every hour brings us nearer to the beginning, and of which no length of time will bring us to the end. Mortification is not virtuous in itself, nor has any other use, but that it disengages us from the allurements of sense. In the state of future perfection, to which we all aspire, there will be pleasure without danger, and security without restraint.'

The princess was silent, and Rasselas, turning to the astronomer, asked him, whether he could not delay her retreat, by shewing her something which she had not seen before.

'Your curiosity,' said the sage, 'has been so general, and your persuit of knowledge so vigorous, that novelties are not now very easily to be found: but what you can no longer procure from the living may be given by the dead. Among the wonders of this country are the catacombs, or the ancient repositories, in which the bodies of the earliest generations were lodged, and where, by the virtue of the gums which embalmed them, they yet remain without corruption.'⁴

'I know not,' said Rasselas, 'what pleasure the sight of the catacombs can afford; but, since nothing else is offered, I am resolved to view them, and shall place this with many other things which I have done, because I would do something.'

They hired a guard of horsemen, and the next day visited the catacombs. When they were about to descend into the sepulchral caves, 'Pekuah,' said the princess, 'we are now again invading the habitations of the dead; I know that you will stay behind; let me find you safe when I return.' 'No, I will not be left,' answered Pekuah; 'I will go down between you and the prince.'

They then all descended, and roved with wonder through the labyrinth of subterraneous passages, where the bodies were laid in rows on either side.

CHAP. XLVIII

Imlac discourses on the nature of the soul¹

'What reason,' said the prince, 'can be given, why the Egyptians should thus expensively preserve those carcasses which some nations consume with fire, others lay to mingle with the earth, and all agree to remove from their sight, as soon as decent rites can be performed?'

'The original² of ancient customs,' said Imlac, 'is commonly unknown; for the practice often continues when the cause has ceased; and concerning superstitious ceremonies it is vain to conjecture; for what reason did not dictate reason cannot explain. I have long believed that the practice of embalming arose only from tenderness to the remains of relations or friends, and to this opinion I am more inclined, because it seems impossible that this care should have been general: had all the dead been embalmed, their repositories must in time have been more spacious than the dwellings of the living. I suppose only the rich or honourable were secured from corruption, and the rest left to the course of nature.

'But it is commonly supposed that the Egyptians believed the soul to live as long as the body continued undissolved, and therefore tried this method of eluding death.'[3]

'Could the wise Egyptians,' said Nekayah, 'think so grosly of the soul? If the soul could once survive its separation, what could it afterwards receive or suffer from the body?'

'The Egyptians would doubtless think erroneously,' said the astronomer, 'in the darkness of heathenism, and the first dawn of philosophy. The nature of the soul is still disputed amidst all our opportunities of clearer knowledge: some yet say, that it may be material, who, nevertheless, believe it to be immortal.'

'Some,' answered Imlac, 'have indeed said that the soul is material, but I can scarcely believe that any man has thought it, who knew how to think; for all the conclusions of reason enforce the immateriality of mind, and all the notices of sense and investigations of science concur to prove the unconsciousness of matter.

'It was never supposed that cogitation is inherent in matter, or that every particle is a thinking being. Yet, if any part of matter be devoid of thought, what part can we suppose to think? Matter can differ from matter only in form, density, bulk, motion, and direction of motion: to which of these, however varied or combined, can consciousness be annexed? To be round or square, to be solid or fluid, to be great or little, to be moved slowly or swiftly one way or another, are modes of material existence, all equally alien from the nature of cogitation. If matter be once without thought, it can only be made to think by some new modification, but all the modifications which it can admit are equally unconnected with cogitative powers.'

'But the materialists,'[4] said the astronomer, 'urge that matter may have qualities with which we are unacquainted.'

'He who will determine,' returned Imlac, 'against that which he knows, because there may be something which he knows not;

he that can set hypothetical possibility against acknowledged certainty, is not to be admitted among reasonable beings. All that we know of matter is, that matter is inert, senseless and lifeless; and if this conviction cannot be opposed but by referring us to something that we know not, we have all the evidence that human intellect can admit. If that which is known may be over-ruled by that which is unknown, no being, not omniscient, can arrive at certainty.'

'Yet let us not,' said the astronomer, 'too arrogantly limit the Creator's power.'

'It is no limitation of omnipotence,' replied the poet, 'to suppose that one thing is not consistent with another, that the same proposition cannot be at once true and false, that the same number cannot be even and odd, that cogitation cannot be conferred on that which is created incapable of cogitation.'

'I know not,' said Nekayah, 'any great use of this question. Does that immateriality, which, in my opinion, you have sufficiently proved, necessarily include eternal duration?'

'Of immateriality,' said Imlac, 'our ideas are negative, and therefore obscure. Immateriality seems to imply a natural power of perpetual duration as a consequence of exemption from all causes of decay: whatever perishes, is destroyed by the solution of its contexture, and separation of its parts; nor can we conceive how that which has no parts, and therefore admits no solution, can be naturally corrupted or impaired.'

'I know not,' said Rasselas, 'how to conceive any thing without extension: what is extended must have parts, and you allow, that whatever has parts may be destroyed.'

'Consider your own conceptions,' replied Imlac, 'and the difficulty will be less. You will find substance without extension. An ideal form is no less real than material bulk: yet an ideal form has no extension. It is no less certain, when you think on a pyramid, that your mind possesses the idea of a pyramid, than that the pyramid itself is standing. What space does the idea of a pyramid occupy more than the idea of a grain of corn? or how can either idea suffer laceration? As is the effect such is the cause; as thought is, such is the power that thinks; a power impassive[5] and indiscerptible.'[6]

'But the Being,' said Nekayah, 'whom I fear to name, the Being which made the soul, can destroy it.'

'He, surely, can destroy it,' answered Imlac, 'since, however unperishable, it receives from a superiour nature its power of duration. That it will not perish by any inherent cause of decay, or principle of corruption, may be shewn by philosophy; but philosophy can tell no more. That it will not be annihilated by him that made it, we must humbly learn from higher authority.'

The whole assembly stood a while silent and collected.[7] 'Let us return,' said Rasselas, 'from this scene of mortality. How gloomy would be these mansions of the dead to him who did not know that he shall never die; that what now acts shall continue its agency, and what now thinks shall think on for ever. Those that lie here stretched before us, the wise and the powerful of ancient times, warn us to remember the shortness of our present state: they were, perhaps, snatched away while they were busy, like us, in the choice of life.'

'To me,' said the princess, 'the choice of life is become less important; I hope hereafter to think only on the choice of eternity.'

They then hastened out of the caverns, and, under the protection of their guard, returned to Cairo.

CHAP. XLIX

The conclusion, in which nothing is concluded

It was now the time of the inundation of the Nile: a few days after their visit to the catacombs, the river began to rise.

They were confined to their house. The whole region being under water gave them no invitation to any excursions, and, being well supplied with materials for talk, they diverted themselves with comparisons of the different forms of life which they had observed, and with various schemes of happiness which each of them had formed.

Pekuah was never so much charmed with any place as the

convent of St. Anthony, where the Arab restored her to the princess, and wished only to fill it with pious maidens, and to be made prioress of the order: she was weary of expectation and disgust, and would gladly be fixed in some unvariable state.

The princess thought, that of all sublunary things, knowledge was the best: she desired first to learn all sciences, and then purposed to found a college of learned women, in which she would preside, that, by conversing with the old, and educating the young, she might divide her time between the acquisition and communication of wisdom, and raise up for the next age models of prudence, and patterns of piety.

The prince desired a little kingdom, in which he might administer justice in his own person, and see all the parts of government with his own eyes; but he could never fix the limits of his dominion, and was always adding to the number of his subjects.

Imlac and the astronomer were contented to be driven along the stream of life without directing their course to any particular port.

Of these wishes that they had formed they well knew that none could be obtained. They deliberated a while what was to be done, and resolved, when the inundation should cease, to return to Abissinia.[1]

FINIS.

Notes

For the explanation of obscure terms or of words of which the meaning has changed significantly since Johnson's time, these Notes refer primarily to *A Dictionary of the English Language*, 4th edn. (1773), which was the last edition to be revised by Johnson himself. Where the form used in *Rasselas* differs from the headword in the dictionary, the headword is included.

There are numerous connections which can be drawn between *Rasselas* and Johnson's broader *oeuvre* (including his conversation, as recorded by James Boswell and others), and the Notes could easily have become bloated with references suggesting that particular viewpoints voiced in *Rasselas* can be taken to have authorial backing. In this regard, I have been highly selective, noting only the most striking correspondences of sense or turn of phrase, while also highlighting issues which Johnson returned to repeatedly.

List of Abbreviations

Adventurer Samuel Johnson, *The Idler and The Adventurer*, ed. W. J. Bate, John M. Bullitt and L. F. Powell, The Yale Edition of the Works of Samuel Johnson, vol. II (New Haven and London: Yale University Press, 1963).

Dictionary Samuel Johnson, *A Dictionary of the English Language on CD-ROM, The First and Fourth Editions*, ed. Anne McDermott (Cambridge: Cambridge University Press, 1996).

Idler Samuel Johnson, *The Idler and The Adventurer*, ed. Bate, Bullitt and Powell.

Life James Boswell, *The Life of Samuel Johnson* (1791), ed. R. W. Chapman (Oxford and New York: Oxford University Press, 1980).

Rambler Samuel Johnson, *The Rambler*, ed. W. J. Bate and Albrecht B. Strauss, The Yale Edition of the Works of Samuel Johnson, vols. III–V (New Haven and London: Yale University Press, 1969).

SJ   Samuel Johnson

Voyage   Samuel Johnson, *A Voyage to Abyssinia*, ed. Joel J. Gold, The Yale Edition of the Works of Samuel Johnson, vol. XV (New Haven and London: Yale University Press, 1985).

CHAP. I
Description of a palace in a valley

1.   *Rasselas . . . Abissinia*: Probably adapted from 'Rasselach' in Job Ludolf's *Historia Aethiopica* (1681), an English version of which SJ owned; Rasselach, according to Ludolf, is a son of the wife of Abyssinian Emperor Basilides (see Donald M. Lockhart, ' "The Fourth Son of the Mighty Emperor": The Ethiopian Background of Johnson's *Rasselas*', *PMLA*, 78 (1963), pp. 517–18). *Voyage* includes a reference to 'Rassela Christos lieutenant general to Sultan Segued' (p. 85), and translates '*ras*' as 'chief' (p. 213). Abyssinia was a country in north-east Africa, occupying the land of modern Ethiopia.

2.   *father of waters*: The Nile, the source of which was much disputed but which, according to *Voyage*, rises in 'a province of the kingdom of Goiama, which is one of the most fruitful and agreeable of all the Abyssinian dominions' (p. 81).

3.   *kingdom of Amhara*: Province of Abyssinia within which was situated, according to *Voyage*, 'the famous rock on which the sons and brothers of the Emperor were confin'd till their accession to the throne' (p. 163). Ludolf's *Historia Aethiopica* includes a genealogical table which lists a fourth child of the emperor who 'Escap'd from the Rock of *Amhara*' (see Lockhart, 'The Fourth Son of the Mighty Emperor', p. 518).

4.   *middle part*: Several travel accounts include descriptions of the Abyssinian royalty's imprisonment in mountainous locations. *Voyage* and Ludolf's *Historia Aethiopica* emphasize the harshness of this custom, but here SJ follows a line of more fanciful, romanticized accounts such as Luis de Urreta's *Historia ecclesiastica, politica, natural y moral de los grandes y remotos Reynos de la Etiopia* (1610) and Giacomo Baratti's *The Late Travels of S. Giacomo Baratti* (1670), in which the place of the royals' confinement is represented as a type of Edenic paradise. Lockhart suggests SJ was particularly indebted to Urreta ('The Fourth Son of the Mighty Emperor', pp. 520–23).

5.   *massy*: 'Heavy; weighty; ponderous; bulky' (*Dictionary*).

6.   *engines*: Machines; 'ENGINE . . . Any mechanical complication,

in which various movements and parts concur to one effect' (*Dictionary*).

7. *solemn elephant*: solemn: 'Awful [i.e. awe-inspiring] . . . Striking with seriousness; sober, serious' (*Dictionary*). Cf. James Thompson's *The Seasons* (1730), which SJ knew well: 'High-raised in solemn theatre around, / Leans the huge elephant: wisest of brutes!' (*Summer*, ll. 720–21).

8. *paces*: 'PACE . . . A measure of five feet' (*Dictionary*).

CHAP. II

The discontent of Rasselas in the Happy Valley

1. *Abissinia*: I.e. the emperor of Abyssinia.

2. *luxury*: 'Delicious fare' (*Dictionary*).

3. *officiousness*: 'Forwardness of civility, or respect, or endeavour. Commonly in an ill sense' (*Dictionary*). See also note 4 to Chap. XXXVIII.

4. *anon*: 'Sometimes; now and then; at other times' (*Dictionary*).

5. *humour*: 'General turn or temper of mind . . . Present disposition' (*Dictionary*).

6. *What . . . animal creation*: Rasselas's ruminations upon the differences between humans and other animals echo SJ's in *Rambler* 41 (III, pp. 221–2).

7. *discovered*: 'To DISCOVER . . . To shew; to disclose; to bring to light; to make visible' (*Dictionary*).

CHAP. III

The wants of him that wants nothing

1. *I shall long . . . happiness*: Cf. *Rambler* 150 (V, pp. 35–6): '[T]he experience of calamity is necessary to a just sense of better fortune; for the good of our present state is merely comparative.'

CHAP. IV

The prince continues to grieve and muse

1. *This first beam of hope . . . his eyes*: The role of hope within human happiness was a recurrent theme for SJ. Cf. particularly *Rambler* 67 (III, pp. 353–8), which is devoted to the issue: 'There is no temper so generally indulged as hope . . . Hope is necessary in every condition . . . Hope is, indeed, very fallacious, and promises what it seldom gives; but its promises are more valuable than the gifts of fortune' (pp. 353–4). Cf. also *Rambler* 203 (V, p. 295): 'Hope is the chief blessing of man'; and SJ's letter of

8 June 1762 to an unidentified correspondent: 'Hope is itself a species of happiness, and perhaps the chief happiness which this world affords' (*The Letters of Samuel Johnson, Volume I: 1731–1772*, ed. Bruce Redford (Oxford: Clarendon Press, 1992), p. 203).

2. *portion*: 'Part of an inheritance given to a child; a fortune' (*Dictionary*).

3. *run*: Ran. SJ gives 'run' as both the 'preterite imperfect and participle passive' forms of the verb in 'A Grammar of the English Tongue' in *Dictionary*.

4. *fatal*: 'Appointed by destiny' (*Dictionary*). See also note 3 to chap. XXVI.

5. *He considered . . . behind it*: SJ regularly commented on the need to use time productively, and, despite his own industriousness, chastised himself for not doing so. See, for example, *Rambler* 108 (IV, p. 212): '[H]e that hopes to look back hereafter with satisfaction upon past years, must learn to know the present value of single minutes, and endeavour to let no particle of time fall useless to the ground'; *Adventurer* 137 (pp. 487–8): 'Much of my time has sunk into nothing, and left no trace by which it can be distinguished, and of this I now only know, that it was once in my power and might once have been improved'; and *Idler* 91 (p. 281): 'Life, however short, is made still shorter by waste of time.'

6. *he passed . . . resolves*: Cf. SJ's pamphlet *The Patriot* (1774): '[M]uch time is lost in regretting the time which had been lost before' (*Political Writings*, ed. Donald J. Greene, The Yale Edition of the Works of Samuel Johnson, vol. X (New Haven and London: Yale University Press, 1977), p. 390).

CHAP. V
The prince meditates his escape

1. *able to return*: There is an ambiguity here, but it is presumably those who have entered through the gate who are not allowed to return to the outside world. This is inconsistent with the description in Chap. I of the performers at the annual visit who are competing in order to remain in the valley; the emperor is also able to come and go.

2. *grate*: The *OED* gives an obsolete sense as 'A barred place of confinement for animals, also, a prison or cage for human beings'; *Dictionary* does not include a definition of 'grate' as a complete cage, but gives 'A partition made with bars placed near to one

another, or crossing each other: such as are in cloysters or prisons.'

3.   *prominence*: 'Protuberance; extant part' – 'extant' in the archaic sense of 'Standing out to view; standing above the rest' (*Dictionary*).

CHAP. VI
A dissertation on the art of flying

1.   *dissertation on the art of flying*: For this chapter – a reworking of the Icarus myth which satirizes the aspirations and pride of inventors and projectors – SJ drew repeatedly on *Mathematical Magick: or the Wonders that may be Perform'd by Mechanical Geometry* (1648) by Bishop John Wilkins (1614–72), a renowned Fellow of the Royal Society and keen would-be aviator. For the identification of SJ's source and the close resemblances between the chapter and Wilkins's projections of a flying chariot and other inventions, see Gwin Kolb, 'Johnson's "Dissertation on Flying" and John Wilkins' "Mathematical Magick"', *Modern Philology*, 47 (1949), pp. 24–31.

2.   *artists*: 'ARTIST . . . The professor of an art, generally of an art manual'; the term carries more elevated connotations than 'artisan', which is defined first as 'Artist; professor of an art' but also as 'Manufacturer; low tradesman' (*Dictionary*).

3.   *subtler*: 'SUBTILE . . . This word is often written *subtle* . . . Thin; not dense; not gross' (*Dictionary*).

4.   *parallel*: 'Line on the globe marking the latitude' (*Dictionary*).

5.   *speculation*: 'Examination by the eye; view' (*Dictionary*).

6.   *volant*: 'Flying; passing through the air' (*Dictionary*).

7.   *All skill . . . he has received*: Cf. *Rambler* 56 (III, p. 299): '[T]he great end of society is mutual beneficence'; and *Adventurer* 137 (p. 489): 'The business of life is carried on by a general co-operation.'

8.   *A flight . . . rolling under them*: Given the setting and what is known of SJ's attitude to contemporary colonial expansion (see Introduction, 'Johnson and European imperialism'), 'northern savages' could be taken to mean European imperialists.

CHAP. VII
The prince finds a man of learning

1.   *to support*: 'To endure any thing painful without being overcome' (*Dictionary*).

2.   *Imlac*: SJ probably took this name from Ludolf's *Historia*

Aethiopica (see note 1 to Chap. I, and Lockhart, ' "The Fourth
Son of the Mighty Emperor" ', pp. 518–19)). Lockhart points
out that the 'Emperor Icon Imlac' appears in Ludolf's work 'in
connection with the establishment of the custom of enforced
exile for the princes' (p. 518).

3.   *rehearsed*: 'To REHEARSE … To repeat; to recite' (*Dictionary*).

CHAP. VIII
The history of Imlac

1.   *To talk … a scholar*: Cf. *A Fragment of the late Dr. Johnson,
on the Character and Duty of an Academick*, included in John
Moir, *Hospitality: A Discourse* (London: 1793): 'An academick
is a man supported at the public cost, and dignified with public
honours, that he may attain and impart wisdom. He is maintained by the public, that he may study at leisure; he is dignified
with honours, that he may teach with weight. The great duty
therefore of an academick is diligence of inquiry, and liberality
of communication' (p. 43). Cf. also *Adventurer* 85 (p. 416): 'To
read, write, and converse in due proportions, is … the business
of a man of letters.'

2.   *terrour*: Presumably 'Fear communicated' (the first sense in
Dictionary) rather than 'Fear received' (the second), given the
association here with 'pomp'.

3.   *Goiama*: Dominion of Abyssinia, mentioned in *Voyage* (p. 81),
and now part of Ethiopia (see note 2 to Chap. I).

4.   *spoiled*: 'To SPOIL … To plunder; to strip of goods'
(*Dictionary*).

5.   *governours of the province*: According to *Voyage*, in Abyssinia,
'The governors purchase their commissions, or to speak properly
their privilege of pillaging the provinces' (p. 214).

6.   *literature*: 'Learning; skill in letters' (*Dictionary*).

7.   *negotiate*: 'To NEGOTIATE … To have intercourse of
business; to traffick; to treat: whether of publick affairs, or
private matters' (*Dictionary*).

8.   *sciences*: 'SCIENCE … Any art or species of knowledge'
(*Dictionary*).

9.   *Surat*: Major trading post on the west coast of India.

CHAP. IX
The history of Imlac continued

1. *pleasing terrour*: Notion associated with the experience of the
    sublime – with 'the strongest emotion which the mind is capable
    of feeling', as Edmund Burke writes in *A Philosophical En-
    quiry into the Origin of our Ideas of the Sublime and Beautiful*
    (1757; ed. David Womersley (London: Penguin, 1998), p. 86).
    Imlac's emotions echo Burke's assertions that 'the ocean is an
    object of no small terror' (p. 102) and that 'terror is a passion
    which always produces delight when it does not press too close'
    (p. 92).

2. *admiration*: 'Wonder; the act of admiring or wondering' (*Dic-
    tionary*).

3. *Agra . . . great Moghul*: Agra is a city in north central India and
    was the capital of the Moghul empire, which was ruled by the
    'great Moghul'. He controlled much of the Indian subcontinent
    from 1526 until the eighteenth century.

4. *Persia . . . magnificence*: Now called Iran, Persia was renowned
    for its ancient ruins, particularly those of its former capital Per-
    sepolis. Among other geographers and travel writers, Thomas
    Salmon describes these 'magnificent Remains', in *The Universal
    Traveller: Or, A Compleat Description of the Several Nations of
    the World*, 3 vols. (London: 1752–3), I, pp. 255–6.

5. *accommodations*: 'ACCOMMODATION . . . In the plural,
    conveniences, things requisite to ease or refreshment' (*Dic-
    tionary*).

6. *Persians . . . social*: A commonplace observation in seventeenth-
    and eighteenth-century accounts of Persia. See, for example, *A
    New and Accurate Description of Persia, and Other Eastern
    Nations*, 2 vols. (London: 1724), a translation of John Chardin's
    account of his travels in the 1660s and 1670s, which includes
    praise of the Persians' 'kindness to Strangers; the Reception and
    Protection they afford them, and their Universal Hospitality' (II,
    p. 123), and a long account of the manner of their visiting 'one
    another regularly on all occasions' (II, p. 131).

7. *Arabia . . . pastoral and warlike*: Imlac echoes many commen-
    tators on 'Arabia' (the Arabian peninsula), such as Laurent
    d'Arvieux, a seventeenth-century traveller who observed that
    the Arabs of the region were concerned 'with nothing but
    their Cattle, following their Princes, going to War, and robbing

Passengers' (*The Travels of the Chevalier d'Arvieux in Arabia the Desart*, 2nd edn. (London: 1732), p. 189).

CHAP. X
Imlac's history continued

1. *dissertation upon poetry*: Imlac's dissertation in this much-discussed chapter has traditionally been taken to be an expression of SJ's own thoughts on poetry, but this has been challenged. Weighing the evidence for each side, Howard Weinbrot concludes that in Imlac SJ creates 'a character whose remarks are different from but related to his own' ('The Reader, the General, and the Particular: Johnson and Imlac in Chapter Ten of *Rasselas*', *Eighteenth-Century Studies*, 5:1 (1971), p. 82).

2. *Wherever I went . . . angelick nature*: Cf. the observation by SJ's friend Hester Lynch Piozzi (formerly Thrale) that SJ's 'idea of poetry was magnificent indeed, and very fully was he persuaded of its superiority over every other talent bestowed by heaven on man. His chapter upon that particular subject in his Rasselas, is really written from the fulness of his heart' (*Anecdotes of the late Samuel Johnson* (London: 1786), pp. 283–4). Several eighteenth-century travel accounts point out the high status of poetry in the East and particularly Persia – see, for example, Salmon's account of the Persians who 'in general seem to have a mighty Gust for Poetry: Every Man of Figure has a Poet in his Family . . . The *Persians* excel in Poetry more than in any other Branch of Learning . . . They mix Verse with all the Prose they write, and in their Conversation will introduce their Rhymes frequently' (*The Universal Traveller*, I, p. 282).

3. *the most ancient poets . . . the best*: Favouring ancient over modern poetry had long been commonplace; for example, in *Reflections upon Ancient and Modern Learning* (1694), William Wotton declared the supremacy of 'Ancient Eloquence and Poetry' to be 'so generally held' that it was 'almost an Heresie in Wit among our Poets to set up any Modern Name against *Homer* or *Virgil, Horace* or *Terence*' (*Critical Essays of the Seventeenth Century*, ed. J. E. Spingarn, 3 vols. (Oxford: Clarendon Press, 1909), III, p. 217). In *Preface to Shakespeare*, SJ suggests the function of antiquity in determining literary value, declaring that 'to works . . . appealing wholly to observation and experience, no other test can be applied than length of duration and continuance of esteem' (*Johnson on Shakespeare*, ed. Arthur Sherbo,

The Yale Edition of the Works of Samuel Johnson, vol. VII (New Haven and London: Yale University Press, 1968), pp. 59–60).

4. *nature and passion . . . the same*: Of the thirteen senses of 'nature' in *Dictionary*, number 7 is most apt: 'The constitution and appearances of things'; 'passion' is defined as 'Violent commotion of the mind'. Imlac's universalism echoes SJ's own; cf., for example, *Adventurer* 99 (p. 431): 'human nature is always the same'; SJ's praise of Shakespeare's characters as 'the genuine progeny of common humanity . . . [who] act and speak by the influence of those general passions and principles by which all minds are agitated' (*Preface to Shakespeare, Johnson on Shakespeare*, ed. Sherbo, VII, p. 62); and *Taxation No Tyranny* (1775): 'Humanity is very uniform' (*Political Writings*, ed. Greene, X, p. 3).

5. *the first excel . . . refinement*: Homer and Virgil were sometimes distinguished in this way. Cf. SJ's 'Life of Dryden': 'In the comparison of Homer and Virgil the discriminative excellence of Homer is elevation and comprehension of thought, and that of Virgil is grace and splendor of diction' (*Lives of the English Poets*, ed. George Birkbeck Hill, 3 vols. (Oxford: Clarendon Press, 1905), I, pp. 447–8).

6. *volumes . . . suspended in the mosque of Mecca*: Seven esteemed poetic works, the 'Sabaa Moallakát', transcribed in gold on Egyptian paper, were, tradition has it, suspended in the mosque at Mecca, as Barthélemi d'Herbelot recounts in *La Bibliothèque Orientale* (Paris: 1697), p. 586. Sir William Jones, whom SJ knew, describes the poems and their suspension in *Poems Consisting Chiefly of Translations from the Asiatick Languages* (Oxford: 1772), p. 183, and he later published a transcription and translation of the poems: *The Moallakát, or Seven Arabian Poems, Which Were Suspended on the Temple at Mecca* (London: 1782).

7. *Whatever is . . . elegantly little*: Cf. Burke's *Philosophical Enquiry*, on which SJ is apparently drawing here, particularly Part II, Section VII 'Vastness' and Part III, Section XIII 'Beautiful objects small'.

8. *idea*: 'Mental image' (*Dictionary*). SJ had firm views on the use of 'idea' – according to Boswell, he 'was at all times jealous of infractions upon the genuine English language' and 'was particularly indignant against the almost universal use of the word *idea* in the sense of *notion* or *opinion*, when it is clear that *idea* can

only signify something of which an image can be formed in the mind. We may have an *idea* or *image* of a mountain, a tree, a building; but we cannot surely have an *idea* or *image* of an *argument* or *proposition*' (*Life*, p. 873). See also note 1 to Chap. XVII.

9. *unexpected instruction*: For SJ's views on literary didacticism, see, for example, *Rambler* 3 (III, pp. 14–15): 'The task of an author is, either to teach what is not known, or to recommend known truths, by his manner of adorning them'; and *Preface to Shakespeare* (*Johnson on Shakespeare*, ed. Sherbo, VII, p. 67): 'The end of writing is to instruct; the end of poetry is to instruct by pleasing.'

10. *The business of a poet ... carelesness*: Cf. *Rambler*, 36 (III, p. 197): 'Poetry cannot dwell upon the minuter distinctions, by which one species differs from another, without departing from that simplicity of grandeur which fills the imagination'; and *Preface to Shakespeare* (*Johnson on Shakespeare*, ed. Sherbo, VII, p. 62): 'In the writings of other poets a character is too often an individual; in those of Shakespeare it is commonly a species.'

CHAP. XI
Imlac's narrative continued

1. *enthusiastic*: 'Vehemently hot in any cause' (*Dictionary*).

2. *By what means ... Supreme Being*: For a report of SJ rereading this passage, see Introduction, note 33.

3. *When ... continually resorting*: Cf. *Voyage* (p. 207): 'The Abyssins were much addicted to pilgrimages into the Holy-Land.'

4. *our religion*: This can be interpreted either generally or as a reference to the religion of Imlac and Rasselas themselves, which is not specified. Christianity was Abyssinia's dominant religion, but it existed alongside Islam, Judaism, and other faiths; the characters' religious allegiances are at no point revealed unambiguously.

5. *awful*: 'That which strikes with awe, or fills with reverence' (*Dictionary*).

6. *That the Supreme Being ... justify*: Cf. SJ's observation in a letter to Boswell:

> We may allow Fancy to suggest certain ideas in certain places, but Reason must always be heard, when she tells us, that those ideas and those places have no natural or necessary relation. When we enter a church we habitually recal to mind the duty of adoration,

but we must not omit adoration for want of a temple; ... the Universal Lord is every where present; and that, therefore, to come to Jona [Iona], or to Jerusalem, though it may be useful, cannot be necessary.

(*The Letters of Samuel Johnson, Volume II: 1773–1776*, ed. Bruce Redford (Oxford: Clarendon Press, 1992), p. 134)

7. *Knowledge ... ideas*: Cf. SJ's remark to Boswell: '[A] desire of knowledge is the natural feeling of mankind; and every human being, whose mind is not debauched, will be willing to give all that he has to get knowledge' (*Life*, p. 324).
8. *policy*: 'The art of government, chiefly with respect to foreign powers ... Art; prudence; management of affairs; stratagem' (*Dictionary*).
9. *Human life ... enjoyed*: A commonplace for SJ. Boswell quotes William Maxwell, an Irish clergyman and friend of SJ, who recalled that SJ 'used frequently to observe, that there was more to be endured than enjoyed, in the general condition of human life' (*Life*, p. 442).

CHAP. XII
The story of Imlac continued

1. *choice of life*: SJ had planned to use this phrase as the work's title (see Introduction, p. xiv).
2. *ancient learning*: Ancient Egypt was considered a culture of great learning – one which had become overshadowed by the reputation of the Greek and Roman scholars it was believed to have inspired. See, for example, Nathaniel Forster, *Reflections on the Natural Foundation of the High Antiquity of Government, Arts, and Sciences in Egypt* (Oxford: 1743), p. 1: 'The High Antiquity of Social Life and Civil Government in Egypt, and the Original Invention of Arts and Sciences by its inhabitants are facts, which, it is well known, are generally attested by the ancient Historians'; and James Burgh's comments on 'Egypt being esteemed the mother of learning and arts, and having a great influence over the other nations' (*Thoughts on Education* (London: 1747), p. 47).
3. *Suez*: Egyptian port at the northern tip of the Red Sea. On Cairo, see note 1 to Chap. XVI.
4. *addressed*: Dictionary gives 'courtship' as a meaning for 'address' as a noun; for the verbal form it gives 'apply to another by words' but not to 'court'.

CHAP. XIII
Rasselas discovers the means of escape

1. *perturbation*: 'Disquiet of mind; deprivation of tranquillity ... Commotion of passions' (*Dictionary*).

2. *conies*: 'CONY ... A rabbit; an animal that burroughs in the ground' (*Dictionary*).

3. *the opinion ... the instinct of animals*: Commonplace developed by numerous authors, classical and modern. Alexander Pope's *An Essay on Man* (1733–4), which SJ criticized as unoriginal, reworks the idea (Book III, 11. 169–90).

4. *Great works ... globe*: Cf. *Rambler* 43 (III, p. 235): 'All the performances of human art, at which we look with praise or wonder, are instances of the resistless force of perseverance: it is by this that the quarry becomes a pyramid, and that distant countries are united with canals.'

5. *Do not ... superstition*: According to Boswell, SJ 'was prone to superstition, but not to credulity. Though his imagination might incline him to a belief of the marvellous and the mysterious, his vigorous reason examined the evidence with jealousy' (*Life*, p. 1399).

CHAP. XIV
Rasselas and Imlac receive an unexpected visit

1. *repose*: 'To place as in confidence or trust: with *on* or *in*' (*Dictionary*).

2. *straggler*: 'A wanderer; a rover; one who forsakes his company; one who rambles without any settled direction' (*Dictionary*).

CHAP. XV
The prince and princess leave the valley

1. *eat*: Dictionary gives the past tense of 'eat' as '*ate*, or *eat*'.

2. *dignity*: 'Rank of elevation' (*Dictionary*).

3. *ruggedness of the commercial race*: Cf. SJ's comments on booksellers in his 'Life of Dryden': 'The general conduct of traders was much less liberal in those times than in our own; their views were narrower, and their manners grosser. To the mercantile ruggedness of that race the delicacy of the poet was sometimes exposed' (*Lives of the English Poets*, ed. Hill, I, p. 407).

CHAP. XVI
They enter Cairo

1. *As they approached ... honourable*: The largest city in Africa, Cairo was renowned in Europe for the diversity of its peoples and its liveliness as a trading post. Richard Pococke, for example, describes the 'great mixture of people in Cairo', how the 'conveniency of water carriage makes Cairo a place of great trade', and the 'great conflux of people to Grand Cairo' (*A Description of the East and Some other Countries*, 2 vols. (London: 1743–5), I, pp. 38–9).

2. *offended*: 'To OFFEND ... To assail; to attack' (*Dictionary*).

3. *traffick*: 'Commerce; merchandising; large trade; exchange of commodities' (*Dictionary*).

4. *acquaintance*: Formally an acceptable plural form: 'the plural is, in some authours, *acquaintance*, in others *acquaintances*' (*Dictionary*).

5. *discovery*: 'The act of revealing or disclosing any secret' (*Dictionary*).

6. *voluptuous*: 'Given to excess of pleasure; luxurious' (*Dictionary*).

7. *In the assembly ... reflection*: Cf. *Adventurer* 120 (pp. 467–8):

> He that enters a gay assembly, beholds the chearfulness displayed in every countenance, and finds all sitting vacant and disengaged, with no other attention than to give or to receive pleasure; would naturally imagine, that he had reached at last the metropolis of felicity, the place sacred to gladness of heart, from whence all fear and anxiety were irreversibly excluded ... [B]ut who is there of those who frequent these luxurious assemblies, that will not confess his own uneasiness, or cannot recount the vexations and distresses that prey upon the lives of his gay companions?
>
> The world, in its best state, is nothing more than a larger assembly of beings, combining to counterfeit happiness which they do not feel, employing every art and contrivance to embellish life, and to hide their real condition from the eyes of one another.

CHAP. XVII
The prince associates with young men of spirit and gaiety

1. *images*: 'IMAGE ... An idea; a representation of any thing to the mind; a picture drawn in the fancy' (*Dictionary*).

2. *Happiness ... uncertainty*: Cf. *Rambler* 53 (III, pp. 287–8): 'To make any happiness sincere, it is necessary that we believe it to

be lasting; since whatever we suppose ourselves in danger of losing, must be enjoyed with solicitude and uneasiness.'

3. *riot*: 'Wild and loose festivity' (*Dictionary*). See also note 7 to Chap. XX.

CHAP. XVIII
The prince finds a wise and happy man

1. *auditory*: 'An audience; a collection of persons assembled to hear' (*Dictionary*).

2. *a sage . . . passions*: In what follows the sage voices notions and uses images (for example, the depiction of human nature as a territory requiring government) which derive from a tradition of English stoical philosophical writing of the seventeenth and eighteenth centuries. For a detailed account of this background, see Gwin Kolb, 'The Use of Stoical Doctrines in *Rasselas*, Chapter XVIII', *Modern Language Notes*, 68 (1953), pp. 439–47.

CHAP. XIX
A glimpse of pastoral life

1. *lowest cataract of the Nile*: The northernmost of the Nile's six stretches of shallows at Aswan, around 550 miles from Cairo. The story assumes a shorter distance, since the journey entails just five days of travelling – two to arrive at the palace in Chap. XX, and three following the break taken there.

2. *She hoped . . . shade*: Nekayah clings to a type of pastoral idyll with which SJ had little patience. Cf. his 'Life of Gay': 'There is something in the poetical Arcadia so remote from known reality and speculative possibility, that we can never support its representation through a long work. A Pastoral of an hundred lines may be endured; but who will hear of sheep and goats, and myrtle bowers and purling rivulets, through five acts?' (*Lives of the English Poets*, ed. Hill, II, pp. 284–5). See also *Rambler* 36 (III, pp. 195–200) for SJ's views on why pastoral representations are found pleasing, and *Rambler* 37 (III, pp. 200–205) for a critique of modern pastoral writing based on golden age Arcadian ideals.

CHAP. XX
The danger of prosperity

1. *habitations of men*: The description which follows of a subtly cultivated but informal landscape evokes contemporary English fashion in gardening, as promoted by eminent landscapers such

as William Kent (1685–1748) and Lancelot ('Capability') Brown (1716–83). SJ was aware of the fashion – in his biography of the poet and gardening enthusiast William Shenstone (1714–63), he describes when Shenstone 'began ... to point his prospects, to diversify his surface, to entangle his walks, and to wind his waters' – undertakings which 'multitudes are contending to do well'. SJ shows reservations over whether 'any great powers of mind' are required 'to plant a walk in undulating curves ... to make water run where it will be heard, and to stagnate where it will be seen' (*Lives of the English Poets*, ed. Hill, III, pp. 350–51).

2. *wantoned*: 'To WANTON ... To move nimbly, and irregularly' (*Dictionary*).

3. *youths and virgins*: In the *Dictionary*, 'youths' are exclusively male and 'virgins' are exclusively female.

4. *laws of eastern hospitality ... to enter*: Cf. *Voyage* (p. 50): '[W]hen a stranger comes to a village, or to the camp, the people are obliged to entertain him and his company according to his rank ... a stranger goes into a house of one he never saw, with the same familiarity, and assurance of welcome, as into that of an intimate friend, or near relation.'

5. *Bassa of Egypt*: The local governor for the Ottoman empire (which took possession of Egypt in 1517). *Dictionary* defines 'Bashaw' ('sometimes written *bassa*') as 'A title of honour and command among the Turks; the viceroy of a province; the general of an army'.

6. *share the plunder with the Bassa*: Cf. the account of corrupt Turkish administration in Egypt in John Campbell's spurious *Travels and Adventures of Edward Brown* (London: 1739), p. 368: 'Oppression and Tyranny runs thro' the whole System of Rule ... The *Bassa* hath vast Demands to satisfy, and in order to have wherewith to satisfy them, it is most evident that he must plunder.'

7. *riot*: 'To RIOT ... To revel; to be dissipated in luxurious enjoyments' (*Dictionary*).

CHAP. XXI
The happiness of solitude

1. *happiness of solitude*: Among SJ's many unfavourable comments on solitary living, cf. particularly *Adventurer* 126 (pp. 471–6), an essay written in opposition to 'specious representations of solitary happiness' (p. 472).

2. *saluted*: 'To SALUTE ... To greet; to hail' (*Dictionary*).

3. *enthusiasm*: 'A vain belief of private revelation; a vain confidence of divine favour or communication' (*Dictionary*).

4. *professed arms*: Entered military service.

5. *riots in scenes of folly*: Cf. *Idler* 32 (p. 101): 'Many have no happier moments than those that they pass in solitude, abandoned to their own imagination, which sometimes puts sceptres in their hands or mitres on their heads, shifts the scene of pleasure with endless variety, bids all the forms of beauty sparkle before them, and gluts them with every change of visionary luxury.'

CHAP. XXII
The happiness of a life led according to nature

1. *The happiness ... nature*: This chapter has often been seen as a satire of Jean-Jacques Rousseau's primitivist philosophy, but SJ's derision can be said to be aimed at a wider body of contemporary espousers of the law of nature. See Gwin Kolb, 'Rousseau and the Background of the "Life Led according to Nature" in Chapter 22 of *Rasselas*', *Modern Philology*, 73:4: 2 (1976), pp. S66–S73.

2. *controvertist*: 'Disputant; a man versed or engaged in literary wars or disputations' (*Dictionary*).

3. *right of society ... duty*: Cf. *Idler* 19 (p. 59): '[M]ankind is one vast republick, where every individual receives many benefits from the labours of others, which, by labouring in his turn for others, he is obliged to repay; ... where the united efforts of all are not able to exempt all from misery, none have a right to withdraw from their task of vigilance, or to be indulged in idle wisdom or solitary pleasures.'

4. *a time when ... his heart*: Cf. *Idler* 38 (pp. 119–20): '[P]erhaps retirement ought rarely to be permitted, except to [some including] ... those who have paid their due proportion to society, and who, having lived for others, may be honourably dismissed to live for themselves.'

5. *Of the present state ... own fault*: Cf. *Adventurer* 120 (pp. 469–70): 'The miseries of life, may, perhaps, afford some proof of a future state ... there will surely come a time, when every capacity of happiness shall be filled, and none shall be wretched but by his own fault.'

6. *not written ... infused at our nativity*: This passage, as noted by Owen Ruffhead in the *Monthly Review* (May 1759), is a translation of Cicero's notion of a law of nature contained in his oration for Milo: see *Cicero: The Speeches*, ed. N. H. Watts

(London: Loeb, 1931), pp. 16–17. Kolb cites Matthew Tindal's *Christianity as Old as the Creation* (London: 1731) and Philip Skelton's *Ophiomaches; or Deism Revealed* (London: 1749) among other possible contexts/targets of SJ's satire ('Rousseau and the Background', pp. S70–S71).

7. *Let them learn ... are happy*: Note that Rasselas had already implicitly dismissed such philosophy by recognizing (in Chap. II) that human happiness and that of other animals have different foundations.

8. *fitness*: A central idea in the philosophy of Gottfried Wilhelm Leibniz (1646–1716), who maintained that everything in the world was right because God had created the best possible system in which parts were associated with the whole according to a principle of fitness. In England, Samuel Clarke (1675–1729) became a prominent English exponent of the idea with works such as *A Discourse concerning the Unchangeable Obligations of Natural Religion, and the Truth and Certainty of the Christian Religion* (1705–6).

CHAP. XXIII
The prince and his sister divide between them the work of observation

1. *as he was yet young*: Rasselas must be approximately thirty-two at this point. SJ may have overlooked how many years he had added to Rasselas's life by this point. On the other hand, as someone averse to ageing, he liked to think of youth as having a long span – in 1762, in his early fifties, he reported that 'Last winter I went down to my native town ... My play-fellows were grown old, and forced me to suspect that I was no longer young' (*Life*, p. 263).

CHAP. XXIV
The prince examines the happiness of high stations

1. *popular*: Common, of the people.
2. *revocation*: 'Act of recalling' (*Dictionary*). The *OED* notes under 'revocation': 'In 17–18th cent. esp. the recall of a representative or ambassador from abroad; also in *letters of revocation*'.
3. *Constantinople*: The capital of the Ottoman empire, officially called Istanbul in SJ's time.
4. *Sultan*: The ruler of the Ottoman empire.
5. *Janisaries*: 'JANIZARY ... One of the guards of the Turkish king' (*Dictionary*). The most highly trained soldiers in the

Turkish army, the Janisaries were known for being hugely powerful and occasionally mutinous. In *Irene* (1749), SJ describes the
'hungry Janizary' who 'burns for plunder, / And growls in private
o'er his idle sabre' (*Poems*, ed. E. L. McAdam and George Milne,
The Yale Edition of the Works of Samuel Johnson, vol. VI (New
Haven and London: Yale University Press, 1985), p. 184).

CHAP. XXV
The princess persues her enquiry with more diligence than success

1. *insinuated herself*: 'To INSINUATE ... To push gently into
   favour or regard: commonly with the reciprocal pronoun' (*Dictionary*).
2. *airy*: 'Gay; sprightly; full of mirth; vivacious; lively; spirited; light
   of heart' (*Dictionary*). See also note 2 to chap. XLIV.
3. *countenance*: 'Patronage; appearance of favour; appearance on
   any side; support' (*Dictionary*).
4. *Answer ... father of waters*: Cf. SJ's censure of a similar entreaty
   in Thomas Gray's 'Ode on a Distant Prospect of Eton College'
   (1747): 'His supplication to father Thames, to tell him who drives
   the hoop or tosses the ball, is useless and puerile. Father Thames
   has no better means of knowing than himself' (*Lives of the
   English Poets*, ed. Hill, III, pp. 434–5).
5. *provinces*: 'PROVINCE ... The proper office or business of any
   one' (*Dictionary*).
6. *the poor ... found*: Cf. *Rambler* 53 (III, p. 284): '[I]n the prospect
   of poverty, there is nothing but gloom and melancholy' – one of
   SJ's many comments on the evils of poverty.
7. *Poverty has ... the morrow*: Cf. *Adventurer* 120 (p. 468): 'There
   is in the world more poverty than is generally imagined; ... great
   numbers are pressed by real necessities which it is their chief
   ambition to conceal, and are forced to purchase the appearance
   of competence and chearfulness at the expence of many comforts
   and conveniences of life.'

CHAP. XXVI
The princess continues her remarks upon private life

1. *allayed*: 'To ALLAY ... To join any thing to another, so as to
   abate its predominant qualities. It is used commonly in a sense
   contrary to its original meaning, and is, to make something bad,
   less bad ... to repress; to abate' (*Dictionary*).

2. *candour*: 'Sweetness of temper; purity of mind; openness; ingenuity; kindness' (*Dictionary*).

3. *fatally*: 'By the decree of fate; by inevitable and invincible determination' (*Dictionary*).

4. *Marriage . . . pleasures*: Cf. SJ's remark that '[e]ven ill assorted marriages were preferable to cheerless celibacy' (*Life*, p. 445).

CHAP. XXVII
Disquisition upon greatness

1. *inferiour desert*: I.e. someone less deserving.

2. *All natural . . . bad and good*: Cf. *Adventurer* 120 (p. 469): 'A good man is subject, like other mortals, to all the influences of natural evil.'

CHAP. XXVIII
Rasselas and Nekayah continue their conversation

1. *familiar*: 'Unceremonious; free, as among persons long acquainted' (*Dictionary*).

2. *siege . . . Jerusalem*: The Romans, under the emperor Titus, besieged and destroyed Jerusalem in AD 70.

3. *thousands and ten thousands . . . revolutions*: Cf. *Life* (p. 477): 'I would not give half a guinea to live under one form of government rather than another. It is of no moment to the happiness of an individual . . . [T]he danger of the abuse of power is nothing to a private man.'

CHAP. XXIX
The debate on marriage continued

1. *collect*: 'To COLLECT . . . To infer as a consequence; to gather from premises' (*Dictionary*).

2. *suffrages*: 'SUFFRAGE . . . Vote; voice given in a controverted point' (*Dictionary*).

3. *Every hour . . . Nile*: Cf. *Rambler* 178 (V, p. 173):

> Providence has fixed the limits of human enjoyment by immoveable boundaries, and has set different gratifications at such a distance from each other, that no art or power can bring them together . . . Of two objects tempting at a distance on contrary sides it is impossible to approach one but by receding from the other; by long deliberation and dilatory projects, they may be both lost, but can never be both gained.

CHAP. XXX
Imlac enters

1. *the sciences first dawned . . . world*: See note 2 to Chap. XII.
2. *civil*: 'Civilised; not barbarous' (*Dictionary*).
3. *my business . . . the present world*: Cf. *Idler* 97 (p. 300): 'He that would travel for the entertainment of others, should remember that the great object of remark is human life'; and SJ's comment on his and Boswell's travels in Scotland: 'our business was with life and manners' (*A Journey to the Western Islands of Scotland*, ed. Mary Lascelles, The Yale Edition of the Works of Samuel Johnson, vol. IX (New Haven and London: Yale University Press, 1971), p. 32).
4. *no mind . . . moments*: Cf. *Rambler* 41 (III, p. 221): 'So few of the hours of life are filled up with objects adequate to the mind of man, and so frequently are we in want of present pleasure or employment, that we are forced to have recourse every moment to the past and future for supplemental satisfactions, and relieve the vacuities of our being, by recollection of former passages, or anticipation of events to come.'
5. *Our passions . . . fear*: Imlac's statement echoes René Descartes's assertion in *Les Passions de l'âme* (1649) that there are six basic human passions of which more particular emotional states are distillates; however, Imlac includes hope and fear, in place of wonder and desire in Descartes's treatise.
6. *pompous*: 'Splendid; magnificent; grand' (*Dictionary*).
7. *fabricks*: 'FABRICK . . . A building; an edifice' (*Dictionary*).
8. *uncertain traditions*: For a discussion of classical speculations on the pyramids' history, and of SJ's acquaintance with these works as well as eighteenth-century accounts, including Pococke's *A Description of the East and Some other Countries*, Aaron Hill's *A Full and Just Account of the Present State of the Ottoman Empire* (London: 1709) and John Greaves's *Pyramidographia: Or A Description of the Pyramids in Ægypt* (London: 1646), see Arthur J. Weitzman, 'More Light on *Rasselas*: The Background of the Egyptian Episodes', *Philological Quarterly*, 48:1 (1969), pp. 45–6.

CHAP. XXXI
They visit the pyramids

1. *great pyramid*: The Great Pyramid of Cheops, the description of which in this and the following chapter is, Weitzman argues, indebted to the accounts by Pococke, Hill and Greaves (see note 8 to Chap. XXX).

2. *measured all its dimensions*: A standard part of a visit to the pyramids both for scholars and interested tourists. Greaves's *Pyramidographia* includes detailed accounts of the measurements of three pyramids (pp. 67–114); Joseph Addison's Mr Spectator recalls making 'a Voyage to *Grand Cairo*, on purpose to take the Measure of a Pyramid' (*Spectator*, no. 1 (1 March 1711), in *The Spectator*, ed. Donald Bond, 5 vols. (Oxford: Clarendon Press, 1965), I, pp. 2–3).

CHAP. XXXII
They enter the pyramid

1. *Those who ... enlarge their desires*: Cf. *Idler* 30 (p. 92): 'The desires of man encrease with his acquisitions; every step which he advances brings something within his view, which he did not see before, and which, as soon as he sees it, he begins to want. Where necessity ends curiosity begins, and no sooner are we supplied with every thing that nature can demand, than we sit down to contrive artificial appetites.'

2. *vanity*: The pyramids had long been regarded as products and symbols of vanity and pride; Weitzman points out that the view goes back to at least Pliny the Elder ('More Light on *Rasselas*', p. 48). Cf. SJ's 'An Essay on Epitaphs', in *Gentleman's Magazine*, 10 (December 1740), p. 593: 'The most ancient Structures in the World, the Pyramids, are supposed to be Sepulchral Monuments, which either Pride or Gratitude erected.'

CHAP. XXXIII
The princess meets with an unexpected misfortune

1. *a troop of Arabs ... overtake them*: SJ probably drew here upon an account of a similar incident in Hill's *A Full and Just Account of the Present State of the Ottoman Empire*, pp. 265–7.

CHAP. XXXIV
They return to Cairo without Pekuah

1. *memorial*: *Dictionary* includes no suitable definition, but *OED* has: 'A statement of facts forming the basis of or expressed in the form of a petition or remonstrance to a person in authority, a government, etc.'
2. *sunk*: For the preterite form of 'sink', *Dictionary* gives both 'sunk' and 'sank' – the latter as an ancient form.

CHAP. XXXV
The princess languishes for want of Pekuah

1. *tempestuous sorrow*: With the discussion of sorrow and its alleviation here, cf. *Rambler* 47 (III, pp. 252–8).
2. *condition*: 'Rank' (*Dictionary*).
3. *convenience*: 'Fitness of time or place' (*Dictionary*).
4. *radical*: 'Primitive; original … Implanted by nature' (*Dictionary*).
5. *Do not … motion*: Cf. *Rambler* 47 (III, p. 258): 'Sorrow … is the putrefaction of stagnant life, and is remedied by exercise and motion'; and *Rambler* 165 (V, p. 111): '[T]he stream of life, if it is not ruffled by obstructions, will grow putrid by stagnation.'
6. *to diffuse*: 'To spread; to scatter; to disperse' (*Dictionary*).

CHAP. XXXVI
Pekuah is still remembered

1. *avocation*: 'The business that calls; or the call that summons away' (*Dictionary*); cf. *Rambler* 47 (III, p. 255): '[S]orrow … must give way, after a stated time, to social duties, and the common avocations of life.'
2. *less*: 'The comparative of little'; 'lesser' is given as a 'barbarous corruption of *less*' (*Dictionary*).

CHAP. XXXVII
The princess hears news of Pekuah

1. *Nubia*: Ancient region consisting of what is now Lower Egypt and northern Sudan.
2. *the monastery … Upper-Egypt*: The retreat of the ascetic St Anthony of Egypt (*c.* 251–356), one of the earliest Christian monks. It was visited by European travellers such as Pococke who describes it in *A Description of the East and Some other Countries*, I, p. 70.

CHAP. XXXVIII
The adventures of the lady Pekuah

1. *meat*: 'Food in general' (*Dictionary*).
2. *sons of Ishmael . . . denied to justice*: I.e. the Arabs, who according to tradition are descended from Ishmael, the exiled son of Abraham and Hagar (Genesis 16:11–15, 21:9–21), and take on the '*late invaders*', the Turks of the Ottoman empire. SJ has the Arab present his people as warriors against colonial oppression; many other contemporary representations portrayed Arabs as inherently belligerent and rapacious. Cf., for example, Charles Thompson, *The Travels of the Late Charles Thompson, Esq; Containing his Observations on France, Italy, Turkey in Europe, The Holy Land, Arabia, Egypt, And many other Parts of the World*, 3 vols. (Reading: 1744), III, p. 366:

    > The *Arabs . . .* are the Descendants of *Ishmael*, of whom the Angel foretold before he was born, that he would *be a wild Man*, and that *his Hand would be against every Man, and every Man's Hand against him*. This is almost literally true of his Posterity even to this Day, many of whom not only make it their Business to attack and plunder Strangers who are unarm'd and defenceless, but are frequently at Variance one with another, and keep up implacable and hereditary Animosities among themselves.

3. *punctuality*: 'Nicety; scrupulous exactness' (*Dictionary*).
4. *officious*: 'Kind; doing good offices' (*Dictionary*).
5. *passenger*: 'A traveller; one who is upon the road; a wayfarer' (*Dictionary*).

CHAP. XXXIX
The adventures of Pekuah continued

1. *the tropick*: The Tropic of Cancer.
2. *river-horses*: Hippopotami.
3. *mermaids . . . credulity*: SJ was probably drawing here on Balthazar Telles's *Historia geral da Ethiopia a alta* (Coimbra: 1660), p. 15, in which earlier ideas of the existence of mermaids and tritons in the Nile are denied (see Lockhart, ' "The Fourth Son of the Mighty Emperor" ', pp. 523–4).
4. *sensitive*: 'Having sense or perception, but not reason' (*Dictionary*).
5. *intercepting*: '*To* INTERCEPT . . . To obstruct; to cut off; to

stop from being communicated; to stop in the progress' (*Dictionary*).

CHAP. XL
The history of a man of learning

1.   *vacation*: 'Leisure; freedom from trouble or perplexity' (*Dictionary*).
2.   *sublime*: 'High in stile or sentiment; lofty; grand ... Lofty of mien; elevated in manner' (*Dictionary*).

CHAP. XLI
The astronomer discovers the cause of his uneasiness

1.   *discovers*: 'To DISCOVER ... To make known; not to disguise; to reveal' (*Dictionary*).
2.   *emersion*: 'The time when a star, having been obscured by its too near approach to the sun, appears again' (*Dictionary*).
3.   *rage of the dog-star ... the crab*: Sirius, the bright star which rises during the 'dog days' of August and was believed to contribute to their heat. In ancient Egypt, the star was also seen to be connected with the annual flooding of the Nile (see note 1 to Chap. XLII). Associations with rage and madness were conventional, as in James Thomson's *Edward and Eleonora* (1739): 'the fiery Dog-star's noxious rage' (III.iv), and Pope's *Epistle to Dr. Arbuthnot* (1735): 'The Dog-star rages! ... / They rave ... and madden round the land' (Il. 3 and 6). The crab is the constellation Cancer, which, like the dog-star, was associated with burning summer heat.
4.   *elemental*: 'Produced by some of the four elements' (*Dictionary*), earth, fire, water and air.

CHAP. XLII
The opinion of the astronomer is explained and justified

1.   *raise the Nile ... inundation*: Flooding from the Nile occurs annually; *Voyage* includes a discussion of the much-debated causes of the phenomenon (pp. 88–9).

CHAP. XLIII
The astronomer leaves Imlac his directions

1.   *Of the uncertainties ... reason*: SJ harboured an intense fear of madness. See, for example, *Life* (p. 49): 'To Johnson, whose supreme enjoyment was the exercise of his reason, the disturbance or obscuration of that faculty was the evil most to be

dreaded. Insanity, therefore, was the object of his most dismal apprehension; and he fancied himself seized by it, or approaching to it, at the very time when he was giving proofs of a more than ordinary soundness and vigour of judgement.'

2. *recollected*: 'To RECOLLECT ... To recover reason or resolution' (*Dictionary*).

CHAP. XLIV
The dangerous prevalence of imagination

1. *prevalence*: 'Superiority; influence; predominance; efficacy; force; validity' (*Dictionary*).

2. *airy*: 'Wanting reality; having no steady foundation in truth or nature; vain; trifling' (*Dictionary*).

3. *He who has nothing ... dominion*: Cf. *Rambler* 5 (III, p. 25): 'Every man is sufficiently discontented with some circumstances of his present state, to suffer his imagination to range more or less in quest of future happiness, and to fix upon some point of time, in which ... he shall find the conditions of his life very much improved'; and *Rambler* 203 (V, p. 291): 'It seems to be the fate of man to seek all his consolations in futurity. The time present is seldom able to fill desire or imagination with immediate enjoyment, and we are forced to supply its deficiencies by recollection or anticipation.'

4. *luscious*: 'Pleasing; delightful' (*Dictionary*).

5. *fantastick*: 'Irrational; bred only in the imagination ... Whimsical; fanciful; capricious; humorous; indulgent of one's own imagination' (*Dictionary*).

CHAP. XLV
They discourse with an old man

1. *prattled*: 'To PRATTLE ... To talk lightly; to chatter; to be trivially loquacious' (*Dictionary*).

2. *physical*: 'Relating to nature or to natural philosophy; not moral' (*Dictionary*).

3. *recreate*: 'To refresh after toil; to amuse or divert in weariness' (*Dictionary*).

4. *Praise ... beyond myself*: Cf. *Idler* 41 (p. 130): '[W]hat is success to him that has none to enjoy it. Happiness is not found in self-contemplation; it is perceived only when it is reflected from another.'

5. *vacancy*: 'Time of leisure; relaxation; intermission; time unengaged ... Listlessness; emptiness of thought' (*Dictionary*).

CHAP. XLVI
The princess and Pekuah visit the astronomer

1.   *stay*: 'To wait; to attend; to forbear to act' (*Dictionary*).
2.   *commerce*: 'Common or familiar intercourse' (*Dictionary*).
3.   *scrupulosity*: 'Doubt; minute and nice doubtfulness' (*Dictionary*).

CHAP. XLVII
The prince enters and brings a new topick

1.   *Variety ... content*: Cf. *Preface to Shakespeare*: '[U]pon the whole, all pleasure consists in variety' (*Johnson on Shakespeare*, ed. Sherbo, VII, p. 67).
2.   *converses*: 'To cohabit with; to hold intercourse with; to be a companion to; followed by *with*' (*Dictionary*).
3.   *probatory*: 'Serving for trial' (*Dictionary*).
4.   *catacombs ... corruption*: SJ may have drawn here upon Hill's account of 'those vast *Catacombs*, wherein the Old *Egyptians* were Embalm'd and Buried, and whose black, horrid Wombs do yet contain a formidable Proof, how long our Humane Bodies may preserve their Substance, when defended by the help of *Art*, from the destructive Power of a *Natural* Corruption' (*A Full and Just Account of the Present State of the Ottoman Empire*, p. 264).

CHAP. XLVIII
Imlac discourses on the nature of the soul

1.   *nature of the soul*: This discussion of the materiality or immateriality and mortality or immortality of the soul reflects lively debates which were ongoing among eighteenth-century philosophers and theologians. SJ's definition of 'soul' – 'The immaterial and immortal spirit of man' (*Dictionary*) – shows that his own position was broadly in line with that which Imlac maintains. For a detailed account of the intellectual context of the chapter, see Gwin Kolb, 'The Intellectual Background of the Discourse of the Soul in *Rasselas*', *Philological Quarterly*, 54 (1975), pp. 357–69.
2.   *original*: Origin (the two terms are synonymous in *Dictionary*).
3.   *it is commonly ... eluding death*: Cf. Greaves's account of 'the Ægyptians, who ... beleeved that *as long as the body endured so long the soule continued with it* [... and therefore would] *keepe their dead imbalmed so much the longer, to the end that*

the soule may for a long while continue' (*Pyramidographia*, p. 45).

4. *materialists*: 'MATERIALIST . . . One who denies spiritual substances' (*Dictionary*).

5. *impassive*: 'Exempt from the agency of external causes' (*Dictionary*).

6. *indiscerptible*: 'Not to be separated; incapable of being broken or destroyed by dissolution of parts' (*Dictionary*).

7. *collected*: While there is no reflexive pronoun here, the most fitting of SJ's definitions is '*To* COLLECT *himself*. To recover from surprise; to gain command over his thoughts: to assemble his sentiments' (*Dictionary*).

CHAP. XLIX
The conclusion

1. *resolved ... to return to Abissinia*: Considerable debate has focused upon the ending, which leaves it unclear whether or not the travellers intend to return to the Happy Valley and, if so, whether they would be admitted. For a weighing up of the evidence, see Gwin Kolb, 'Textual Cruxes in *Rasselas*', in *Johnsonian Studies*, ed. Magdi Wahba (Cairo: Société Orientale de Publicité Press, 1962), pp. 257–62.

PENGUIN CLASSICS

KING SOLOMIN'S MINES
H. RIDER HAGGARD

'There at the end of the long stone table ... sat Death himself'

Onboard a ship bound for Natal, adventurer Allan Quartermain meets Sir Henry Curtis and Captain John Good. His new friends have set out to find Sir Henry's younger brother, who vanished seeking King Solomon's legendary diamond mines in the African interior. By strange chance, Quartermain has a map to the mines, drawn in blood, and agrees to join the others on their perilous journey. The travellers face many dangers on their quest – the baking desert heat, the hostile lost tribe they discover and the evil 'wise woman' who holds the secret of the diamond mines. *King Solomon's Mines* (1885) is a brilliant work of adventure romance that has gripped readers for generations.

In his preface Giles Foden considers Haggard's treatment of the cultural stereotypes of the time, while Robert Hampson's introduction discusses the explorations and empire building that inspired Haggard's writing. This edition also includes further reading, an appendix and notes.

'Enchantment is just what Rider Haggard exercised ... his books live today with undiminished vitality' Graham Greene

Edited with an introduction and notes by Robert Hampson
Preface by Giles Foden

PENGUIN CLASSICS

THE LIFE OF SAMUEL JOHNSON
JAMES BOSWELL

'Johnson, to be sure, has a roughness in his manner, but no man alive has a more tender heart'

In Boswell's *Life of Samuel Johnson*, one of the towering figures of English literature is revealed with unparalleled immediacy and originality. While Johnson's *Dictionary* remains a monument of scholarship, and his essays and criticism command continuing respect, we owe our knowledge of the man himself to this biography. Through a series of wonderfully detailed anecdotes, Johnson emerges as a sociable figure with a huge appetite for life, crossing swords with other great eighteenth-century luminaries, from Garrick and Goldsmith to Burney and Burke – even his long-suffering friend and disciple James Boswell. Yet Johnson had a vulnerable, even tragic, side and anxieties and obsessions haunted his private hours. Boswell's sensitivity and insight into every facet of his subject's character ultimately make this biography as moving as it is entertaining.

Based on the 1799 edition, Christopher Hibbert's abridgement preserves the integrity of the original, while his fascinating introduction sets Boswell's view of Samuel Johnson against that of others of the time.

Edited and abridged with an introduction and notes by Christopher Hibbert

PENGUIN CLASSICS

THE JOURNALS OF CAPTAIN COOK

'They crowded so thick round the boats …
that it was some time before we could get room to land'

These *Journals* record the historic meeting between two worlds as Europe's
greatest navigator made the first contact with many of the peoples of the Pacific.
In three extraordinary expeditions, Cook charted the entire coast of New Zealand
and eastern Australia, and made detailed descriptions of Tahiti, Tonga and many
previously unknown islands. Cook's journals display the skill and courage with
which he faced the continuous dangers of uncharted seas and endeavoured to
form relationships with the peoples he encountered. While he had an eighteenth-
century Englishman's imperial self-assurance, Cook writes of 'native' cultures with
striking sympathy and respect to create a truly compelling and revealing account of
these momentous voyages of discovery.

This edition, abridged from the Hakluyt Society's definitive four-volume
collection and preserving Cook's idiosyncratic spelling, makes this inimitable
personal account of his nine years of voyaging accessible to the general reader.
Philip Edwards provides an introduction to each voyage and a postscript on the
controversy surrounding Cook's death.

Selected and edited with introductions by Philip Edwards

PENGUIN CLASSICS

A JOURNAL OF THE PLAGUE YEAR
DANIEL DEFOE

> 'It was a most surprising thing, to see those Streets,
> which were usually so thronged, now grown desolate'

In 1665 the Great Plague swept through London, claiming nearly 100,000 lives. In *A Journal*, written nearly sixty years later, Defoe vividly chronicled the progress of the epidemic. We follow his fictional narrator through a city transformed: the streets and alleyways deserted; the houses of death with crosses daubed on their doors; the dead-carts on their way to the pits. And he recounts the horrifying stories of the citizens he encounters, as fear, isolation and hysteria take hold. *A Journal* is both a fascinating historical document and a supreme work of imaginative reconstruction.

This edition contains a new introduction, an appendix on the Plague, a topographical index and maps of contemporary London, and reproduces Anthony Burgess's original introduction.

'The most reliable and comprehensive account of the Great Plague that we possess'
Anthony Burgess

'Within the texture of Defoe's prose London becomes a living and suffering being'
Peter Ackroyd

Edited with an introduction by Cynthia Wall

PENGUIN CLASSICS

ROBINSON CRUSOE
DANIEL DEFOE

> 'A raging wave, mountain-like, came rowling a-stern of us
> … we were all swallowed up in a moment'

The sole survivor of a shipwreck, Robinson Crusoe is washed up on a desert island. In his journal he chronicles his daily battle to stay alive, as he conquers isolation, fashions shelter and clothes, first encounters another human being, and fights off cannibals and mutineers. With *Robinson Crusoe*, Defoe wrote what is regarded as the first English novel, and created one of the most popular and enduring myths in literature. Written in an age of exploration and enterprise, it has been variously interpreted as an embodiment of British imperialist values, as a portrayal of 'natural man', or as a moral fable. But above all it is a brilliant narrative, depicting Crusoe's transformation from terrified survivor to self-sufficient master of his island.

This edition contains a full chronology of Defoe's life and times, explanatory notes, glossary and a critical introduction discussing *Robinson Crusoe* as a pioneering work of modern psychological realism.

'Robinson Crusoe has a universal appeal, a story that goes right to the core of existence' Simon Armitage

Edited with an introduction and notes by John Richetti

read more   🐧

PENGUIN CLASSICS

GULLIVER'S TRAVELS   JONATHAN SWIFT

'I felt something alive moving on my left Leg ... when bending my Eyes downwards as much as I could, I perceived it to be a human Creature not six Inches high'

Shipwrecked and cast adrift, Lemuel Gulliver wakes to find himself on Lilliput, an island inhabited by little people, whose height makes their quarrels over fashion and fame seem ridiculous. His subsequent encounters – with the crude giants of Brobdingnag, the philosophical Houyhnhnms and brutish Yahoos – give Gulliver new, bitter insights into human behaviour. Swift's savage satire views mankind in a distorted hall of mirrors as a diminished, magnified and finally bestial species, presenting us with an uncompromising reflection of ourselves.

This text, based on the first edition of 1726, reproduces all its original illustrations and includes an introduction by Robert Demaria, Jr., which discusses the ways *Gulliver's Travels* has been interpreted since its first publication.

'A masterwork of irony ... that contains both a dark and bitter meaning and a joyous, extraordinary creativity of imagination. That is why it has lived for so long' Malcolm Bradbury

Edited with an introduction by Robert DeMaria, Jr

THE STORY OF PENGUIN CLASSICS

Before 1946 ... 'Classics' are mainly the domain of academics and students; readable editions for everyone else are almost unheard of. This all changes when a little-known classicist, E. V. Rieu, presents Penguin founder Allen Lane with the translation of Homer's *Odyssey* that he has been working on in his spare time.

1946 Penguin Classics debuts with *The Odyssey*, which promptly sells three million copies. Suddenly, classics are no longer for the privileged few.

1950s Rieu, now series editor, turns to professional writers for the best modern, readable translations, including Dorothy L. Sayers's *Inferno* and Robert Graves's unexpurgated *Twelve Caesars*.

1960s The Classics are given the distinctive black covers that have remained a constant throughout the life of the series. Rieu retires in 1964, hailing the Penguin Classics list as 'the greatest educative force of the twentieth century.'

1970s A new generation of translators swells the Penguin Classics ranks, introducing readers of English to classics of world literature from more than twenty languages. The list grows to encompass more history, philosophy, science, religion and politics.

1980s The Penguin American Library launches with titles such as *Uncle Tom's Cabin*, and joins forces with Penguin Classics to provide the most comprehensive library of world literature available from any paperback publisher.

1990s The launch of Penguin Audiobooks brings the classics to a listening audience for the first time, and in 1999 the worldwide launch of the Penguin Classics website extends their reach to the global online community.

The 21st Century Penguin Classics are completely redesigned for the first time in nearly twenty years. This world-famous series now consists of more than 1300 titles, making the widest range of the best books ever written available to millions – and constantly redefining what makes a 'classic'.

The Odyssey continues ...

The best books ever written

PENGUIN CLASSICS

SINCE 1946

Find out more at www.penguinclassics.com